Karolinum Press

ABOUT THE AUTHOR

Jaroslav Hašek (1883–1923) was a Czech writer and one of the most important interwar authors.

At the turn of the 20th century he wandered around Europe leading a vagrant and bohemian life and became acquainted with Czech anarchists, an experience which affected his later work and thinking. Initially, he focused mainly on sketches, short travel pieces and humorous stories for magazines, most of which were written in Prague's pubs. Later he worked as an editor for several anarchist magazines.

Having voluntarily joined the army in 1915, he left for the Galician front and later joined the Czechoslovak Legion in Russia, and in 1918 the Red Army in which he became a commissar. From 1920 till his death he lived in Czechoslovakia.

He wrote about 1,200 short stories. His participation in the world war and in the Russian revolution lies at the foundation of the future direction of his work in which the grotesque often intertwines with tragedy. In his most famous novel, *The Good Soldier Švejk: and His Fortunes in the World War* (1921–23, the most translated book in Czech literature), Hašek explores the conflicts within society, while also compassionately describing the frailty of a man fighting in vain for his ideals. Employing parody and the grotesque, he addresses fundamental issues in modern philosophy and sociology as well as aesthetics and literary science, which have earned this work the reputation as "the bible of humor." There have been several film adaptations of *The Good Soldier Švejk* as well as stage adaptations (e.g. from Bertold Brecht's).

MODERN CZECH CLASSICS

Jaroslav Hašek

Behind the Lines Bugulma and Other Stories

Translation from the Czech by Mark Corner

KAROLINUM PRESS 2016

KAROLINUM PRESS
Karolinum Press is a publishing department
of Charles University in Prague
Ovocný trh 3, 116 36 Prague 1
Czech Republic
www.karolinum.cz

Cover illustration by Jiří Grus
Designed by Zdeněk Ziegler
Set and printed in the Czech Republic
by Karolinum Press

Cataloging-in-Publication Data is available
from the National Library of the Czech Republic

ISBN 978-80-246-3287-2 (pbk)
ISBN 978-80-246-2013-8 (hbk)
ISBN 978-80-246-3371-8 (ebk)

COMMANDING OFFICER, TOWN OF BUGULMA

It was the beginning of October, 1918. That was when the Revolutionary Military Council on the left bank of the Volga in Simbirsk gave me the news. I had been made Commanding Officer of the Town of Bugulma. I spoke with the Chairman, one Kayurov: ‘Are you quite sure that Bugulma is already in our hands?’

‘No specific information has been received,’ was the response I got. ‘I’d be surprised if it was in our hands right now, but by the time you get there I have no doubt it will be.’

‘I take it that I’ll have an escort?’ I asked in a quiet voice. ‘One other thing – how do I get to this Bugulma? I mean to say, where is it?’

‘You’ll have an escort, twelve men strong. As for your other question, look at a map. Do you think I’ve got nothing better to do than worry about where some wretched Bugulma is?’

‘Just one further question, Comrade Kayurov. When will I get some money to cover my travelling and living expenses?’

My words evoked a bout of exasperated hand-waving. ‘You must be out of your mind. The journey will certainly take you through several villages where you’ll be given food and drink, and when you get to Bugulma you can impose a levy.’

My escort was waiting for me below in the guardhouse. Twelve stout Chuvash fellows with hardly a word of Russian, which meant that they were unable to put me in the picture as to whether they were conscripts or volunteers. From the way they looked, at once jovial and terrifying, it was a safe guess that they were volunteers, men who would stop at nothing.

When I had received my papers and a power of attorney making it crystal clear that every citizen between Simbirsk and Bugulma must cater to all my needs, I set off with my expeditionary force and we boarded a steamer which took us by way of the Volga and its tributary the Kama as far as Chistopol.

There were no incidents in the course of our journey, save for the fact that one of my Chuvash escorts fell overboard in a drunken stupor and drowned. That left me with eleven. When we clambered off the steamer at Chistopol one of the remaining Chuvashes offered to round up some horse-drawn carts and then failed to return. So now they were down to ten. They managed to let me know that the disappearing Chuvash, must have gone to see how things were with his parents in Montazmo, about forty versts, or twenty-five miles, away.

When at last, after lengthy inquiries concerning the whereabouts of Bugulma and how to get there, I'd made a note of everything the local citizenry had to tell me, the rest of the Chuvashes secured some carts and we set off along the abysmal mud-soaked by-ways of that region towards Krachalga, Jelanovo, Moskovo, Gulokovo and Abashevo. The composition of these villages was pure Tartar, with the exception of Gulokovo, which is shared between Tartars and Cheremisses.

Seeing that there was a terrible enmity between the Chuvashes, who had adopted Christianity some fifty years earlier, and the Cheremisses, who have remained devoutly pagan to this day, Gulukovo was the scene of a minor mishap. Armed to the teeth as they inspected the village, the Chuvashes proceeded to drag before me the mayor, one Davledbai Shakir, who had in his hand a cage with three white squirrels in it. One of the Chuvashes, the one with the largest smattering of Russian, turned to me and put me in the picture:

'Chuvashes Orthodox one year, Orthodox ten years, thirty years, fifty years – Cheremisses pagan swine.'

Snatching the cage with the white squirrels out of Davledbai Shakir's hands, he went on:

'White squirrel their god – one, two, three gods. This man priest, this man go leap with squirrels, go leap and pray to them. You now baptise him…'

So menacing was the look on the Chuvash faces that I ordered water to be brought and sprinkled it over Davledbai Shakir, quietly spouting some mumbo jumbo as I did so. Then I let him go.

My fine fellows then proceeded to skin the gods of the Cheremisses. I can assure one and all that you can make a fine soup out of a Cheremiss deity.

After that it was the turn of the local mullah, Abdullah by name, to visit me. He expressed delight at the fact that we'd eaten those squirrels. 'Everyone must have something to believe in,' he said, 'but to believe in squirrels, such a thing is sheer beastliness. The way they scurry from one tree to another and make their messes when they're in a cage – is that any way for a god to carry on?' He brought us lavish helpings of roast mutton and three geese, assuring us that if there were to be a Cheremiss uprising during the night the Tartars would be with us to a man.

In the event nothing happened because, as Davledbai Shakir pointed out when he turned up to see us off in the morning, there are plenty of other squirrels in the forest. In the end we moved on through Abashevo and in the evening, without further mishap, we arrived in Little Pisetsnitse, a Russian village some twenty versts from Bugulma. The local inhabitants were very well informed about what was going on in Bugulma. The counter-revolutionary Whites had abandoned the town without a fight three days earlier. The Soviet army had come to a halt on the other side of the town, afraid to enter in case it was ambushed.

Inside the town no one was in control. Meanwhile the mayor and his entire council had been waiting for two days with bread and salt to welcome whoever deigned to enter.

I sent on ahead the Chuvash who was the least worst Russian speaker, and by morning we had all moved forward to Bugulma.

On the outskirts of the town we encountered a disorderly crowd of people coming to meet us. The mayor was there with a loaf of bread on a platter and a saucerful of salt.

He made a speech expressing the hope that I would have mercy on his town. It made me think of myself as Jan Žižka at the gates of Prague, especially when I noticed the schoolchildren in the procession.

I made a long speech in return thanking him, cutting a slice of bread and dosing it in salt. I made a point of saying that I had not come to mouth platitudes but with one aim in mind: Peace, Quiet and Order. I concluded proceedings with a kiss for the mayor and a handshake for the representative of the Orthodox clergy, before setting off for the town hall, where a headquarters had been assigned to me as Commanding Officer of Bugulma.

The next item of business was to have Order No. 1 posted up. It read as follows:

Citizens!

I should like to thank each and every one of you for the heartfelt and sincere welcome you gave me and for your hospitality with the bread and salt. Preserve at all times these ancient Slavic customs. I have no wish to denigrate them in any way, but please bear in mind at the same time that I have been appointed Commanding Officer of this town, a position which means that I too have my obligations.

In the light of this fact I hereby request you, dear friends, to relinquish all your weapons at the town hall, where your Commanding Officer has his headquarters, at around noon tomorrow. It is not my wish to threaten anyone, but you will be aware of the fact that this is a town under siege.

I might add that I was to have imposed a levy upon this town. However, I hereby announce that no dues will have to be paid.

Gašek

At noon the next day the square was overflowing with armed men. Well over a thousand of them armed with rifles. Some were even dragging a machine gun along.

The eleven of us might easily have been overwhelmed by this armed tide, but they had come only in order to hand over their weapons. They went on doing so long into the evening, while I shook each one of them by the hand and said a few friendly words.

In the morning I had Order No. 2 printed and posted up:

Citizens!

I would like to thank all the inhabitants of Bugulma for the punctilious manner in which they carried out Order No. I.

Gašek

I went to my bed peacefully that day, unaware that there was a Sword of Damocles hanging over my head in the shape of the Tver Revolutionary Regiment.

As I have already pointed out, the Soviet army was positioned on the other side of Bugulma some fifty versts to the south and didn't dare to enter the town itself, fearing an ambush. In the end, however, they received an order from the Revolutionary Military Council in Simbirsk to occupy the town, come what may, and secure it as a base for the Soviet forces operating to the east of the town.

And so it came about that Comrade Yerokhimov, commander of the Tver Revolutionary Regiment, arrived that very night to occupy and subdue Bugulma, when I had already been its godfearing Commanding Offficer for three days and had been carrying out my duties to the general satisfaction of all sections of the populace.

Once the Tver Revolutionary Regiment had 'penetrated' the town, they fired salvos into the air as they passed through the streets, encountering no resistance except for my bodyguard of two Chuvashes. These were woken up while on guard duty at the door of the Commanding Officer's HQ and refused Comrade Yerokhimov entry to the town, hall when he arrived, revolver in hand, to take possession of it at the head of his regiment.

The Chuvashes were taken prisoner and Yerokhimov stormed into my office-cum-bedroom.

'Hands up,' he called out, flush with victory and with his revolver pointing right at me. I calmly did as he said.

'Who might you be, then?' the commander of the Tver Regiment asked.

'I am the Commanding Officer of Bugulma.'

'Would that be White or Soviet?'

'Soviet. May I put my hands down now?'

'You may. However, I would ask you in accordance with the rules of war to hand over your command to me without further ado. I am the one who has conquered Bugulma.'

'But I am the one who was appointed Commanding Officer,' I protested.

'To hell with your appointment. You first have to conquer the place.'

'I'll tell you what,' he added, having taken a moment to bring out his magnanimous side, 'I am prepared to make you my second-in-command. If you don't agree I'll have you shot within five minutes.'

'I've no objection to becoming your second-in-command,' I replied, and summoned my orderly. 'Vasily, put on the samovar. We will take tea with the new Commanding Officer of this town. He has just conquered Bugulma....'

Sic transit gloria mundi.

SECOND-IN-COMMAND TO THE COMMANDING OFFICER, TOWN OF BUGULMA

My first task was to free my two captured Chuvashes and then make up for sleep lost due to the coup in the town. At some time before noon I woke up to discover that all my Chuvashes had mysteriously disappeared, leaving a note stuffed into one of my boots. I could barely make it out:

Comrade Gašek. Going seek much help here there all around. Comrade Yerkokhimov bashka-khawa *(off with head).*

The second thing I discovered was that Comrade Yerokhimov had been in a sweat from early morning over the wording of his first official pronouncement to the inhabitants of Bugulma.

'Comrade Second-in-Command', he said to me, 'Do you think this will hit the mark?' He produced a piece of paper from a pile of draft orders covered in scrawl. Lines had been crossed out and new words inserted. It now read:

To all citizens of Bugulma! This very day, following the fall of Bugulma, I have taken over as your Commanding Officer. I am hereby dismissing your former Commanding Officer from his post on grounds of incompetence and cowardice and am appointing him my second-in-command.

Yerokhimov, Commanding Officer of Bugulma

'That seems to take care of everything,' I said approvingly. 'What are your plans now?'

'First of all,' he intoned solemnly, 'I shall order the mobilisation of horses. Then I shall have the mayor of the town shot. I shall take ten hostages from the bourgeoisie and hold them in prison for the duration of the Civil War. After that I shall carry out a house-to-house search of the town and prohibit any independent traders. That's enough for one day. I'll think up something else for tomorrow.'

'Please permit me to point out,' I said, 'that while I have nothing whatever against rounding up horses, I must protest in the strongest possible terms against shooting the town's mayor. The man made me welcome with bread and salt.'

Yerokhimov leapt to his feet. 'He might have welcomed you, but he hasn't yet been to see me.'

'That can be fixed,' I said. 'We'll send for him.' I sat down at the desk and wrote:

Commanding Officer's HQ
Town of Bugulma
No. 2891
Centre of Army Operations

To the Mayor of Bugulma

I order you to present yourself immediately to the new commanding officer of the town. You will bring bread and salt in accordance with ancient Slavic tradition.

Commanding Officer of the Town: Yerokhimov
Second-in-command: Gašek

When Yerokhimov had signed it he added:

Otherwise you will be shot and your house burned to the ground.

'You can't add something like that to official documents,' I told Yerokhimov. 'You'll make them invalid.'

I copied it out once more with the original wording, before having it signed and sending it off via an orderly.

'Furthermore,' I said to Yerokhimov, I am completely opposed to the idea of keeping ten members of the bourgeoisie in prison until the Civil War is over. That's a matter for the Revolutionary Tribunal alone to decide.'

'We are the Revolutionary Tribunal,' said Yerokhimov solemnly, 'the town is in our hands.'

'There you're mistaken, Comrade Yerokhimov. What are we but a couple of old sweats living down among the dregs? Nothing but the Commanding Officer of a town and his aide-de-camp. The Revolutionary Tribunal is appointed by the Revolutionary Military Council of the Eastern Front. Do you want them to put you up against a wall?'

'Have it your own way,' replied Yerokhimov with a sigh. 'Even so, surely no one can keep us from a rummage through the town.'

'As to that there's a Decree of 18th June of this year,' I replied, 'stating that a general house-search can be carried out only with the agreement of the local Revolutionary Committee or Council. Since such a body does not yet exist, we had better put your rummage on a back burner.'

'What an angel you are,' said Yerokhimov tenderly, 'without you I would have been sunk. But surely we can go ahead with putting an end to this free marketeering.'

'Those who engage in trade and frequent the bazaars,' I explained, 'are mostly country people. They are muzhiks who don't know how to read or write. First they'll have to learn to be literate. Only then will they be able to read our official notices and know what they're on about. Our first task is to teach an illiterate population the arts of reading and writing. That's the way to make them understand what we want from them. Then we'll be able to issue orders, perhaps for your mobilisation of horses. Tell me, Comrade Yerokhimov, why are you so set upon rounding up all those horses? Perhaps you want to convert the Tver Revolutionary Infantry Regiment into a cavalry division. Are you aware that such a development would have to go through the Military Arrangements Directorate of the Left-bank Formation?'

'Right again, Comrade Gašek,' said Yerokhimov with another sigh. 'What do I do, then?'

'Teach the people of the Bugulma region to read and write,' I replied. 'As for me, I'll check what your fellows have been up to and whether they've managed to sort anything out in the way of billeting.'

I left him and took a turn around the town. The Tver Revolutionary Regiment was behaving decently. No one was being pushed around. In fact the regiment had made friends with the local inhabitants to the point of drinking their tea and having borscht, fish soup and dumplings cooked for them. They in turn shared sugar and baccy with their hosts. In short, all was as it should be. I moved on to take a look at Little Bugulma, where the first battalion of the regiment had been quartered. There too I found everything hunky dory. The men were drinking tea, eating borscht and minding their manners. I came back late in the evening and spotted a freshly posted official notice at the corner of the square. It read:

To the whole Population of Bugulma, Town and Region

I order everyone in the town and surrounding area who has not yet learned to read and write to do so within three days. Anyone found to be illiterate after this time will be shot.

Commanding Officer of the Town: Yerokhimov

When I found Yerokhimov he was sitting with the mayor of the town, who had turned up not only with the bread and salt, which was carefully laid out upon the table, but also several bottles of old Lithuanian vodka. The high-spirited Yerokhimov had the mayor in an embrace. As soon as he saw me he shouted:

'Have you read how I took your advice? I carried the notice to the printing press in person and had the director look down the barrel of my gun. "Print this at once, sweety-pie, or I'll shoot you on the spot, you cur." That gave him the shakes, the scoundrel. He was trembling while he read the notice, and the notice made him tremble even more. And then I go *Bang*! *Bang*! into the ceiling. And the upshot was he printed the notice, printed it handsomely. To know how to read and write, that's what it's all about. You issue an order, everyone can read what it says, they get the message, they're content. That's the way, isn't it, Mr Mayor. Wet your whistle, Comrade Gašek.'

I turned the offer down.

'Will you have a drink or won't you?' he shouted.

I took out my revolver and shot the bottles of Lithuanian vodka. Then I pointed the weapon at my superior officer and said in a commanding voice: 'Go and lie down at once, or else….'

'On my way, sweety-pie, my heart's delight. Just enjoying ourselves. Having a bit of fun. Making whoopee.' I escorted Yerokhimov out and put him to bed. Then

I went back to the mayor and said to him: 'It's a first offence, so I'm letting you off. Run along home and be thankful that you got off so lightly.'

Yerokhimov slept until two in the afternoon the next day. When he woke up he sent for me, gave me an uneasy look and remarked: 'I have a feeling that you wanted to shoot me yesterday.'

'Quite right,' I replied. 'I was merely saving you from something worse. I'm referring to what the Revolutionary Tribunal would have done to you when it learned that the town's Commanding Officer had been sozzled.'

'You won't say anything about it, sweety-pie, will you? It'll never happen again. I'm going to teach the people to read and write….'

The evening saw the first deputation of muzhiks. They came from the Karlagin region. There were six grandmas of between sixty and eighty years of age, and six grandpas of the same vintage.

They threw themselves at my feet. 'Don't imperil our very souls, little father, *batyushka*. We cannot learn to read and write in three days. We haven't the heads for it. We ask you as our saviour to have mercy on this our foolishness.'

'The order is invalid,' I said. 'It is all the fault of that twerp Yerokhimov, the town's Commanding Officer.'

Further deputations arrived during the night, but by morning fresh notices had been posted all over the town and neighbouring districts. They read as follows:

To every citizen living in Bugulma, Town and Region

I am making it known that I have dismissed the Commanding Officer of this town, Comrade Yerokhimov, and have taken up office again myself. I hereby declare his Order no. 1 and Order No. 2 concerning the elimination of illiteracy within three days to be invalid.

Commanding Officer of Bugulma: Gašek

I could allow myself to take such a step because during the night the Petersburg Cavalry Regiment arrived in town, brought by my Chuvashes in order to take care of Yerokhimov.

THE VIA DOLOROSA

The former Commanding Officer of the town, Yerokhimov, the man I had relieved of the burden of office, now issued an order to the whole of the Tver Revolutionary Regiment instructing it to leave the town in battle formation and encamp just outside it. He then paid me a farewell visit. I assured him that if he or his regiment tried to cause any further unpleasantness, I would have them disarmed and send him before the Revolutionary Military Tribunal of the Front. Clearly we were putting our cards on the table.

For his part, Comrade Yerokhimov assured me in the sincerest manner that as soon as the Petersburg Cavalry Regiment had withdrawn from the town he would have me strung up on a hill overlooking Little Bugulma, where I could be seen from all directions.

We shook hands and parted company the best of friends.

After Yerokhimov's departure with his regiment I had to find comfortable quarters for the Petersburg Cavalry, which was made up for the most part of volunteers, and spruce up the barracks for them. My first priority was to do everything within my power to ensure that those fine Petersburg fellows had a good time in Bugulma and were not going to turn against me one fine day.

But whom should I send to clean the barracks, scrub the floors and tidy everything up? Obviously people with nothing to do.

The trouble was that every one of the local inhabitants had work to do. I racked my brains for a long time and then I remembered that there was a large group of nuns in the vicinity of the town at the Convent of the Most Holy Mother of God. They did nothing all day except pray and tell tales about each other.

So I wrote the following official letter to the abbess:

Bugulma Military Command Centre
No. 3896 Centre of Army Operations
To Comrade Abbess of the Convent
of the Most Holy Mother of God

Send fifty virgins from your convent at once. They are to be placed at the disposal of the Petersburg Cavalry Regiment. Send them directly to the barracks.

Supreme Commander of the Town: Gašek

The letter was despatched and some thirty minutes later a most enchanting and powerful peal of bells could be heard coming from the convent. Howls and drones from every bell in the Convent of the Most Holy Mother of God were echoed by the bells of the town church.

My orderly informed me that the archpriest of the main church was asking whether I would receive him accompanied by the local clergy. No sooner had I nodded affably than the office was overrun by bearded priests. They had a chief spokesman who delivered the following address:

'Comrade Sir Commander, I come to you not only as a representative of the local priesthood but in the name of the Holy Orthodox Church in its entirety. Do not ravage the innocent convent maidens. We have just had a message from the convent that you want fifty nuns for the Petersburg Cavalry Regiment. Remember the One who is above us.'

'The only thing above us right now is the ceiling,' I replied with a whiff of sarcasm, 'as far as the nuns are concerned, it must be as I say. I need fifty of them for the barracks. If it turns out that thirty are enough to do the job, I will send the other twenty back. On the other hand if fifty proves insufficient for the task, I will requisition a hundred from the convent, two hundred, three hundred. I couldn't give a fig. As for you, Gentlemen, I am obliged to point out that you are poking your beards into official matters, and for that I am compelled to fine you. Each one of you will supply me with three pounds of wax candles, a dozen eggs and a pound of butter. I authorise you, citizen archpriest, to arrange with the abbess when she will deliver me those fifty nuns. Tell her that the need for them is an urgent one and she will get them back later on. Not one will go missing.'

The Orthodox clergy left my office in very low spirits.

In the doorway the most senior one, with the largest helping of beard and hair, turned to me and said:

'Remember that the Lord of Hosts is looking down on us.'

'I beg your pardon,' I said, 'in your case you will bring five pounds of candles instead of three.'

It was one of those glorious afternoons that October brings. A severe frost had set in, adding a crusty coating to the cursed Bugulma mud. The streets began to fill up with people flocking to the main church. Grave and solemn was the tolling of the town and convent bells. They were not sounding the alarm as they had been earlier in the day, but were summoning Bugulma's faithful to a *via dolorosa* (procession of the cross).

Only in the worst of times was there such a procession in Bugulma. When Tartars had the town under siege, when there were epidemics of plague or smallpox, when war broke out, when the Tsar had been shot and right now. Softly mournful is the tone of the bells, as if they want to burst into tears.

The gates of the convent open and out they come with their icons and banners. Four of the oldest nuns with the abbess in the lead are carrying a large icon of considerable weight.

The image of the Most Holy Mother of God looks down from the icon in dumb dismay. Behind it march an army of nuns, young and old, in their all-black uniforms, their marching song a biblical text: 'And they led him away to be crucified. They crucified him and two thieves with him, one on each side and the Lord between them.' At the same moment the orthodox clergy emerge from the church, their vestments embroidered in gold, followed by the laity dragging along heavy icons.

Both processions converge in a clamour of 'Christ lives, Christ reigns, Christ is victorious!'

Now the whole crowd begins singing: 'I know that my Redeemer lives, and that He will stand upon the earth on the last day.'

The procession passes by the church and turns towards the official residence of the town's Commanding Officer, where I have already made preparations to suit the occasion.

In front of the building stands a table covered with a white cloth, on which lies a loaf of bread and salt in a salt cellar. In the right-hand corner stands an icon flanked by burning candles.

When the procession arrives in front of my official residence, I go out solemnly and ask the abbess to accept bread and salt as proof that I hold no hostile intent. In addition I invite the Orthodox clergy to take a slice of bread. One by one they come to kiss the icon.

'Men and women of the Orthodox Church,' I begin with solemnity, 'I would like to thank you for a splendid and unusually eye-catching Procession of the Cross. I saw it today for the first time in my life and it has left an impression which will last until my death. Seeing this chanting crowd of nuns here, I am reminded of those early Christian processions in the time of Emperor Nero. I take it that some of you have read *Quo vadis?* In any case, men and women of Orthodoxy, I do not wish to try your patience any further. I asked for only fifty nuns, but now I see that the whole convent is here, which should enable us to get everything over and done with more quickly. I would therefore ask the maidens from the nunnery to follow me to the barracks.'

The crowds stand bare-headed before me and sing in response: 'The heavens declare the glory of God and the firmament sheweth His handiwork. Day unto day uttereth speech and night unto night sheweth knowledge.'

The abbess steps forward in front of me. Her aged chin trembles as she asks me: 'In the name of the Lord God of Hosts, what are we going to do there? Do not plunge your soul into ruin.'

'Hosts of Orthodoxy,' I shout to the crowd, 'There are floors to be scrubbed and a barracks to be made clean so that the Petersburg Cavalry Regiment can be quartered there. Now let's get on with it.'

The crowd follow in my wake and by evening, with such a workforce of willing hands, the barracks are in perfect order.

In the evening a comely young nun brings me a small icon and a note from the aged abbess containing the simplest of sentences: 'I am praying for you.'

Now I sleep in peace because I know that to this day, among the old oak forests of Bugulma, there is a Convent of the Most Holy Mother of God, where an old abbess lives and prays for a sinner like me who is nothing worth.

A STRATEGIC HITCH

At the end of October 1918 I received the following order in my Bugulma HQ from the Revolutionary Military Council of the Eastern Front:

The Light Artillery (16th Division) is on the march. Sledges must be prepared for transporting the division to the front.

The telegram was nothing if not disconcerting. What exactly was this division? How many thousand men did it have? Where would I find all those sledges it needed? I have to confess that in matters military I was not among the initiated. Austria had failed to provide me with the basics of a military education and had fought tooth and nail to exclude me from any inner sanctum where the arts of warfare might be revealed.

They ejected me from the officers' school of the 91st Infantry Regiment at the start of the war and later on ripped off my stripes as a one-year volunteer. While my former comrades-in-arms were being rewarded with titles like 'cadet' and 'ensign', enabling them to fall like flies on all fronts, I was parking my carcase in military detention centres at Budějovice and Most nad Litavou. When they finally released me, intending to have me sent straight to the front with the march companies, I hid in a haystack and survived the departure of three of these units. After that I made out that I had epilepsy and that brought me close to being shot, a fate I avoided only by announcing of my own free will that I was ready to go to the front. From that very moment Fortune smiled on me and when, en route to Sambor, I managed to procure for Lieutenant Lukas an apartment with a charming Polish landlady and superb cooking thrown in, my reward was promotion to orderly officer.

Later on, somewhere beneath Sokal, lice attacked the battalion commander. I caught the lot one by one by rubbing mercury ointment into him on the spot in the trenches. For that I received the Grand Silver Medal for Gallantry.

Throughout all this no one deigned to initiate me into the mysteries of the art of warfare. To this day I haven't the faintest idea how many regiments make up a battalion or into how many companies you can chop up a brigade. And now here I was in Bugulma, supposed to be *au fait* with the number of sledges needed to transport a division of light artillery. None of my Chuvashes could answer the question either, for which failing they received a suspended sentence of three days in prison. If they lighted upon the solution within one year, their offence would be wiped from the record.

I summoned the mayor of the town and said to him sternly, 'It has come to my attention that you are concealing from me how many men make up a division of light artillery.'

His first response was speechlessness. His second was to fling himself onto the ground, embrace me by the legs and wail: 'Have mercy on me and stay your mighty hand, for no such slander ever escaped my lips.'

I hoisted him off the ground and treated him to tea and tobacco. Then I released him with the assurance that in this case he had convinced me of his innocence.

He went home and sent me a roast suckling-pig with a dishful of pickled mushrooms. I wolfed down the lot, but was no nearer to knowing how many men there were in a division and how many sledges they'd be needing.

I sent for the Commanding Officer of the Petersburg Cavalry Regiment and let the matter quietly bubble to the surface in the course of our conversation.

'It's a rum thing,' I said, 'how High Command is always changing the number of men in the light artillery divisions. With the Red Army finally taking shape, it is awkward to see that shape changing. You wouldn't happen to know, Comrade Commander, how many men there used to be in a division before the latest changes?'

He released phlegm before words: 'We are cavalry men and that means we have nothing to do with artillery. Besides, I don't even know how many men I ought to have in my own regiment. The point is they never sent me any instructions on the matter. What they told me was to make up a regiment, so I set about recruiting men. One had a friend, the friend had another friend, and so the thing went on growing. When I've got a fair whack of them, I'll call them a brigade. What are a bunch of Cossacks compared to one of our brigades?

He left me knowing no more than I'd known before he arrived. Then came the last straw. I received the following telegram from Simbirsk. It began:

Threats faced by our forces on frontline mean you appointed Commander of the Front. Should enemy penetrate our positions on River Ik, withdraw our regiments to Klučevo-Bugulma line. Convene Extraordinary Committee for Defence of Town and defend till last man. Begin evacuation of town once enemy within fifty versts. Mobilise inhabitants under fifty-two and distribute weapons. Choose moment to blow up railway bridge over Ik and at Klučevo. Scout land using armoured train and blow up railway track.

I let the telegram drop from my hand. Pulling myself together as best I could after the first wave of shock, I read the thing to the very end:

Put hoisting and loading machinery to flames. Destroy whatever cannot take. Wait for reinforcements, see to billeting, make sure supplied. Organise rail transportation of ammunition to our positions. Publish magazine in Tartar and Russian to placate inhabitants. Appoint Committee of the Revolution. Failure to execute these orders or deviation from specific demands punishable in accordance with wartime regulations.
Revolutionary Military Council of the Eastern Front

Evening was falling but I left the lamps unlit. I stayed slumped in my armchair, and when later on the moon peeked through my window it saw the same man in the same chair, holding the same telegram in his hand, an idiotic look on his face as he stared at the twilight of his office.

And that's how the morning sun found me too. As dawn broke the icon hanging in the corner could put up with it no longer. It fell off the wall and smashed itself to smithereens.

The Chuvash on guard outside the door popped his head inside and wagged a threatening finger at the icon. 'You bad woman. Go drop drop. Make chap to wake up.'

As morning broke I took a portrait of my dear departed mother out of my pocket, tears welling up in my eyes, and whispered: 'Mama dear! Remember how years ago we lived together at number 4 Milešovská Street in Prague-Vinohrady. You never thought then that within fifteen years your poor little boy would have to withdraw regiments to the Klučevo-Bugulma line, blow up railway bridges over the River Ik and at Klučevo, blow up railway tracks, put hoisting and loading gear to the flames and hold out in defence of the town until the last man falls – I'm just giving you a selection of my duties here. Why didn't I follow your advice to became a Benedictine monk when I first fluffed my exams? I would have known inner peace. I would have officiated at holy mass and drunk the monastery wine.'

As if by way of answer a suspicious rumbling sound began in the south-east of the town and continued a second and a third time.

'The artillery is carving us up nicely,' an orderly officer fresh from the front informed me. 'Kapel's men are across the Ik and advancing against us on the right flank. There's a Polish division with them. The Tver Regiment is falling back.

I sent the following order to the front:

If General Kapel's forces across Ik and advancing with Polish division against our right flank, cross to the other side of Ik and advance against their left flank. Am sending Petersburg Cavalry to attack rear.

I summoned the commanding officer of the Petersburg Cavalry Brigade. 'They've burst through our positions,' I explained to him, 'which creates just the space we need to get them in the rear and seize the whole of that Polish division.'

'Just so,' replied the Commanding Officer of the Petersburg Cavalry Brigade. He left with a salute.

I made my way to the telegraph machine and sent Simbirsk the following message:

Stunning victory. Positions on Ik overrun. Our attack from all sides. Cavalry mounting enemy rear. Heaps of prisoners.

BUGULMA'S GLORY DAYS

What a fool that Napoleon was. Look at how the poor fellow beavered away trying to unearth the secrets of strategic thinking. He pored through every available tome in order to come up with his theory of the unbroken front. He was at the military schools in Brienne and Paris, had his military tactics all worked out, and what happened? He met his Waterloo.

Many followed his example and they all received a thrashing. Seen in the light of Bugulma's days of triumph, it seems to me that all those victories of Napoleon, from the occupation of Cape L'Aiquiletta through Mantova, Castiglione, Aspern and all the rest are stuff and nonsense. There's no doubt in my mind that if Napoleon had acted as I did at Waterloo he'd have given Wellington the boot.

Back then Blücher launched himself against Napoleon's right flank. Napoleon should then have done just what I did at Bugulma, when we had the volunteer corps of General Kapel and the Polish division on *our* right flank.

Why didn't he order his guard to fall on Blücher's *left* flank, the very thing I did myself in my order to the Petersburg Horsemen?

These horsemen worked wonders, because Russia is a boundless expanse and a few miles are neither here nor there. They rode as far as Menzelinsk and arrived in the region of Chishma and God knows where else to the rear of the enemy. Then they drove all before them, turning the victory of their foes into a defeat.

Unfortunately most of our enemies were able to withdraw to Belebey and Buguruslan, while the rest, driven from behind by the Petersburg horsemen, ended up no more than fifteen versts from Bugulma.

As for the Tver Revolutionary Regiment with Comrade Yerokhimov at the helm, they spent Bugulma's glory days in constant retreat before a vanquished enemy.

Evenings saw them disperse themselves among all the Tartar villages, where they wolfed down the geese and chickens before retreating once again near to Bugulma and then doing some more dispersing to other villages before finally entering the town in full working order.

They came hurrying to me from the printing works with the news that the Commanding Officer of the Tver Regiment, one Yerokhimov, was threatening the director with a revolver in an attempt to have some order and a proclamation printed.

I took my four Chuvashes in tow, threw in two Brownings and a Colt revolver and took myself off in the direction of the printing works, where I found the director in his office. He was seated in one chair and Comrade Yerokhimov was seated a hair's breadth away in the other. The director was in a somewhat uncomfortable position, because his visitor was holding a revolver against the man's temple and was saying: 'To print or not to print. That is the question.'

Then I heard the director of the printing works answer. It was a manful response.

'I'm not going to print it. It just can't be done, my dear sir,' whereupon his neighbour with the revolver implored him:

'Print it, my soul's delight, my little love-bird, print it, I beg of you.'

When they saw me, a clearly embarrassed Yerokhimov hurried over to embrace me and offer me a hearty handshake. Then he turned to the director and said with a wink: 'I haven't seen him in a long time, so we've spent the last half hour entertaining one another.'

I noticed that the director spat and made his feelings clear by growling: 'Some entertainment!'

'Word has it,' I said to Yerokhimov, 'that you want to have something printed. A proclamation or an order – something of that kind. Would you be so kind as to let me take a look at the text?'

'It was just a joke, Comrade Gašek, just a little horseplay,' Yerokhimov replied in a downhearted tone of voice. 'I didn't want to make anything out of it.'

I took the original from the table. This was what he'd wanted to have printed and what no citizen of Bugulma ever got to read. If they had, they would certainly have been surprised by what Yerokhimov had in store for them. The original document read as follows:

Proclamation Number One

Having returned at the head of the victorious Tver Revolutionary Regiment, I am hereby making it known that the government of this town and surrounding district is in my hands. I am putting in place an Extraordinary Revolutionary Tribunal, whose President will be myself. It will hold its first meeting tomorrow, where the matter under discussion will be one of the utmost importance. In the light of his counter-revolutionary and conspiratorial tendencies, the Commanding Officer of the town, Comrade Gašek, will stand before the Extraordinary Revolutionary Tribunal. Should he be condemned to go before a firing squad, the sentence will be carried out within twelve hours. All inhabitants should be mindful of the fact that any kind of rebellion will be punished on the spot.

My friend wanted to serve up the following order as an additional notice:

Order number 3

The Extraordinary Revolutionary Tribunal of the Bugulma Military District hereby announces the following decision of the Extraordinary Revolutionary Tribunal, namely that the former Commanding Officer of this town, one Gašek, has been shot as a counter-revolutionary and conspirator against the Soviet government.

Yerokhimov

President, Extraordinary Revolutionary Tribunal

'Nothing but a bit of hanky panky, my soul's delight,' said Yerokhimov soothingly, 'Would you like to have my revolver? Go on, take it, how could I possibly shoot anyone with it?'

I was struck by his mild tone of voice. Then I turned round and saw that my four Chuvashes, with hard and dangerous looks on their faces, were pointing their rifles right at him.

I ordered them to shoulder arms and relieved Yerokhimov of his revolver, while he fixed his childlike blue eyes on me and said quietly, 'Am I under arrest or free to go?'

I smiled. 'You are a simpleton, Comrade Yerokhimov. No one gets put away for little jokes like that. You yourself admitted that it was nothing serious. But there is something else which you should be arrested for. I am referring to your shameful return. The Poles had already been smashed to smithereens by our Petersburg Cavalry when you were retreating before them until you were back inside the town. Are you aware of the fact that I have a telegram from Simbirsk in which the Tver Revolutionary Regiment is ordered to drape its old revolutionary banner in new victory laurels? Take back this revolver that you handed over to me, but on one condition, that you leave this town at once, overcome the Poles and bring in prisoners. You will do so without harming so much as a hair on their heads. Otherwise you'll be in hotter water than you could ever handle, let me make that clear. I'm sure you understand that we cannot make fools of ourselves in the eyes of Simbirsk. I have already telegraphed them that the Tver Regiment has taken heaps of prisoners.

Then I struck the table with my fist: 'So where are these prisoners of yours? Where are they?'

Thrusting the fist like a fencing foil under his nose, I added in a voice of terrifying menace, 'Just you wait, I'll make you pay for this! Do you have anything to say before you set off with your regiment to fetch prisoners? Have I made it clear to you that I am the Commanding Officer at the front, the one in charge here?

Yerokhimov stood straight as a post, with only his eyes registering a flicker of agitation. Finally he saluted and declared: 'I will crush the Poles and deliver prisoners this very evening. Thank you, sir.'

I handed him his revolver, shook his hand and bid him a warm farewell.

Yerokhimov was magnificently true to his word. By morning the Tver Regiment had started to bring in prisoners. The barracks was full of them and we couldn't work out where to put them.

I went to inspect them and nearly fainted from shock. Instead of Poles Yerokhimov had collected peasants – Tartars living in the villages. The Poles had failed to hang around for the Tver Regiment's surprise attack and instead had turned their cowardly tails on it.

NEW DANGERS

It was simply impossible to persuade Comrade Yerokhimov that the local population of peaceful Tartars were not Poles. When I gave the order that all the supposed 'prisoners' being rounded up by Yerokhimov in the villages were to be set free, he felt insulted. He headed for the military telegraph office of the Petersburg Cavalry Brigade and attempted to send the following telegram to the Revolutionary Military Council of the Eastern Front at Simbirsk:

After three days action can report opposition forces crushed by Tver Revolutionary Regiment. Enemy losses huge. 1,200 Whites captured, then released by Commanding Officer of Bugulma. Hereby request despatch of special commission to investigate whole affair. Commanding Officer Comrade Gašek completely unreliable, counter-revolutionary, in contact with enemy. Request organise Extraordinary Commission for Combating Counter-Revolution.

Yerokhimov, Commanding Officer,
Tver Revolutionary Regiment

The head of the telegraph office accepted the telegram from Comrade Yerokhimov, assuring him that it would be sent just as soon as the line was free. Then he took to his sledge and came to see me.

'By St. George, Father Gašek, we're done for now', he said to me, his expression emptied of all hope, 'Just look at this.' He passed across to me Comrade Yerokhimov's telegram.

I read it and stuffed it calmly into my pocket. The man in charge of the telegraph office began scratching his head while blinking rather nervously. 'You must admit that my position is complicated, highly complicated.' According to the provisions of the People's Commissariat, it is my duty to accept any telegrams from regimental commanders. And you apparently wish me not to send this one. I didn't come here in order to hand the telegram over to you. I came here to acquaint you with its contents and give you the opportunity of sending another telegram challenging Comrade Yerokhimov.'

I explained to the head of the telegraph office that I held the People's Commissariat for War in the highest regard, but that unlike them we were in the thick of the action. 'This is the front. I am the Commanding Officer on the front line and that means I can do as I like. My orders are that you accept as many telegrams from Comrade Yerokhimov as he is disposed to write. However, I forbid you to send them. You must bring them here to me at once.'

'For the moment,' I finished up, 'I am letting you remain at liberty, but I should warn you that the slightest deviation from our agreed programme will have consequences beyond your darkest imaginings.'

I had some tea with him while we chatted about more mundane matters, and then took my leave with a warning that he must tell Yerokhimov his telegram had been sent.

After dinner the Chuvash on guard duty informed me that our entire military HQ had been surrounded by two companies of the Tver Revolutionary Regiment and that Comrade Yerokhimov was delivering a speech proclaiming the End of Tyranny.

And sure as rain Comrade Yerokhimov himself arrived in my office a short while later, accompanied by ten soldiers who stationed themselves at the door with bayonets fixed.

Without so much as a word to me Comrade Yerokhimov began to post his men at key locations around the office.

'You'd better go here, you go there, you stay in this position, you go to that corner there. I want you by the table, you over there by that window and you take the other window. I want you to stay close to me.'

I rolled a cigarette and found myself surrounded by a sea of bayonets by the time I had lit it. This gave me the chance to observe what Comrade Yerokhimov's next move might be.

It was clear from his look of uncertainty that he didn't know the answer himself. He made his way to the table with official documents, tore one or two of them up and then set himself moving about the office for a while, a soldier with bayonet keeping pace at his heels.

His comrades in arms, who were standing facing me from all corners of the room, wore serious expressions until one of them, green in years, asked: 'Comrade Yerokhimov, may we smoke?'

'Smoke away,' answered Yerokhimov and parked himself in front of me.

I offered him tobacco and rolling papers. He puffed away and inquired in a hesitant tone: 'Simbirsk tobacco, is it?'

'From the Don region,' came my short reply, while I began to leaf through the papers on the table as if he wasn't present.

An awkward silence followed. It was finally broken by Comrade Yerokhimov saying to me in a quiet voice:

'What would your reaction be, Comrade Gašek, if I were to be made the President of an Extraordinary Commission for Combating Counter-Revolution?'

'I would have no choice but to offer you my congratulations,' I replied, 'Perhaps you would like another cigarette?'

He lit it and went on in a voice tinged with sadness:

'You can take it for granted, Comrade Gašek. And assuming that I have indeed been made President of an Extraordinary Commission for Combating Counter-Revolution appointed by the Revolutionary Military Council of the Eastern Front....'

He stood up at this point and a strong tone entered his voice: '...You're at my mercy.'

'First things first,' I said in a quiet voice. 'Show me your authorisation.'

'Authorisation be damned,' said Yerokhimov, 'I can arrest you without any.'

I smiled.

'Be so kind as to go back to your seat quietly, Comrade Yerokhimov. The samovar will be here in a moment and then we'll have a little chat about appointment procedures to Extraordinary Commissions to Combat Counter-Revolution.'

I turned around to face Yerokhimov's escort. 'As for you, you've no business being here. Away with you. Comrade Yerokhimov, tell them to make themselves scarce.' Yerokhimov managed a sheepish smile: 'Fly off, my little lovebirds, and take the men outside with you.

They're to go home too.'

When they'd all gone and the samovar had replaced them, I said to Yerokhimov: 'If you really had authorisation you could now have me arrested and shot and generally do to me whatever you'd imagined you could do in your capacity as President of an Extraordinary Commission.'

'I'll get that authorisation,' came the quietly-spoken response from Yerokhimov. 'You needn't have any doubt on that score, sweetheart.'

I removed Yerokhimov's ill-fated telegram from my pocket and put it in front of him.

'How the hell did you get hold of that?' Yerokhimov protested in grief-stricken tones. 'That should have been sent on its way a long time ago.'

'The point is this, my friend,' I replied in affable tones, 'all army telegrams have to be signed by the Commanding Officer of the front, and that's why they brought your telegram to me for signature. If you really insist on sending it, then in spite of everything I've said I'm willing to sign it and you can take it to the telegraph office yourself. You see, I don't have anything to fear from you.'

Yerokhimov picked up his telegram and tore it to pieces amidst wails and sobs. 'My dearest friend, my oldest bean, it was just a little jest, nothing meant by it, my only friend, forgive me.'

We took tea together until two a.m. We spent the night in a single bed, took more tea together in the morning and I furnished him with a quarter pound of the best tobacco for his journey home.

Eight days on from the Glorious Days of Bugulma, and still not a whisker of the Petersburg Cavalry Regiment. Comrade Yerokhimov, who had become very solicitous in his visits since our last encounter, made daily utterances concerning his suspicion that the Petersburg Cavalry Regiment had gone over to the enemy. He proposed that I i) pronounce them traitors to the Republic ii) telegraph Trotsky in Moscow with details of their criminal act of desertion iii) organise a Revolutionary Tribunal of the Front and summon before it the head of telegraph office of the Petersburg Cavalry, because the man must have been aware of what was going on. And if he wasn't aware, he should be summoned anyway, because he was the one in charge of communications.

Comrade Yerokhimov's bullying campaign was nothing if not punctilious. He arrived at eight in the morning and hounded me until half past nine. Then he presented himself for a new bout of intimidation which lasted from two until four in the afternoon. In the evening he agitated against the Petersburg Cavalry until ten or eleven, this time over tea.

He would circle round my office with his head hung during these visits, while he kept repeating in despondent tones: 'What a terrible thing and what dishonour it brings to our Revolution. We must telegraph. We must be in direct touch with Moscow!'

I comforted him by saying that everything would turn out for the best. 'There will come a time, Comrade Yerokhimov, when you will see the Petersburgers come back.'

Meanwhile I received the following telegram from the Revolutionary Military Council of the Eastern Front:

Specify number of prisoners taken. Last telegram re magnificent victory at Bugulma unclear. Despatch Petersburg Cavalry to Third Army at Buguruslan. Notify full compliance with orders in previous telegram. Indicate how many copies of magazine published in Tartar and Russian. Inform of publication's title. Send courier with detailed account of your activities. Position Tver Revolutionary Brigade where effective. Arrange appeal to White Army forces to defect by dropping leaflets from aircraft. Mistakes or failure to comply with all demands punishable as per wartime regulations.

This one was still sinking in when the next arrived:

Do not send courier. Stand by for Inspector from Eastern Front and head of political wing of Revolutionary Military Council with Soviet member, Comrade Morozov. They have every authority.

Comrade Yerokhimov was present at this moment. When I'd read through the second telegram I passed it across. I wanted to see what effect such a fearsome inspection committee would have on him. After all, it was just what he'd been pressing for.

One could observe a man in a state of mental turmoil. As an opportunity to take sweet revenge on me, it was worth embracing. But the radiant smile which lit up his face did not stay there. Its place was taken by the anxious appearance of a disturbed mind.

'You're done for, sweetheart,' he said in a doleful voice. 'That boisterous head of yours will have to be pushed off its perch.'

He set off on a walking tour of the office singing in wistful tones as he went:

How long, dashing head above
Will I be carrying you, my love?

Then he took a seat before continuing: 'If I were in your place I'd make a run for it. Head for Menzelinsk and then from there to Osa and from Osa to Perm and then catch me if you can, you dunderheads! Just hand over command of the town and the front to me and I'll sort everything out.'

'I don't think there's anything for me to be concerned about,' I said.

Yerokhimov whistled knowingly. 'Nothing for him to be concerned about! Has he prepared any horses for the off? No. Has he got reservists from the local population? He has not. Has he imposed a contribution on the town? No sign of it. Have counter-revolutionaries been thrown into gaol? No throw. Has he even found a counter-revolutionary to throw? None found. Now let him tell me this: Has he at least managed to have a priest shot - or any member of the merchant class? Not one. Has he had the former rural police chief shot? Not he. What about the former mayor of the town? Alive and kicking or six feet under? Kicking. You see how things are. And yet you persist in saying that you've nothing to fear. Things don't look at all good for you, my dear.'

He resumed his walking tour of the office whistling the same song as he went:

How long, dashing head above
Will I be carrying you, my love?

He grasped his head in his hands while I calmly watched the cockroaches swarming over the warm part of the wall near the stove. Then Yerokhimov set off in a run, going from window to window and back to the door, still with his head in his hands and intoning as he went: 'What can he do? What can he do? The little love-bird is finally through. He's bound to be dead, his boisterous head must come off its perch and land before you!'

After five minutes of running he sat down on a chair and with a clueless look on his face began to say:

'There's just nothing to be done. If you could only say that the gaol was full, but what have you got there? Not a single prisoner. If you could only show the inspectors that you'd found some compound where counter-revolutionaries were hiding out and had razed it to the ground. But you've nothing to show them, not a dicky bird. You haven't even searched the town house by house. Let me tell you in all honesty, much as I like you personally I can't avoid a very low opinion of you professionally.'

He rose to his feet, strapped on his belt and tucked his revolver inside it together with a Caucasian knife half a metre in length. He took my hand and assured me that he only wished to help, that he didn't know exactly how to do so but that he would surely come up with something.

After he'd left I telegraphed the following reply to Simbirsk:

Ascertaining prisoner numbers. Moving front, lack of maps, inhibit account of Bugulma victory. Inspectors to verify on spot. Hitch re magazine in Tartar and Russian. No Tartar typesetters, lack Russian type, Whites taken printing presses. If air squadron based Bugulma, can airdrop appeals to White Army. Currently waiting planes. Tver Revolutionary Regiment here back-up against ambush.

I slept the sleep of the just. Morning came and with it Yerokhimov, who said he'd thought up a way of saving me. A group of them had been working on it all night.

He led me out of town to a former brickworks where I found myself facing members of the 5th Company of the Tver Revolutionary Regiment on guard duty. They were standing there with bayonets fixed, shouting at anyone trying to get past them: 'You there, off to the left; no one passes here.'

Right in the middle of this spot a little surprise awaited me in the form of three graves, the earth used to cover the bodies still fresh. The 'headstone' of each grave came in the form of a post with a board fixed for the inscription. The inscription above the first grave read as follows:

Interred here is the former rural police chief. He was shot in October 1918 as a counter-revolutionary.

Then came the inscription above the second grave:

Interred here is the local priest. He was shot in October 1918 as a counter-revolutionary.

And then the inscription above the third grave:

Here lies duly interred the mayor of the town. He was shot in October 1918 as a counter-revolutionary.

My legs almost gave way under me as, supported by Comrade Yerokhimov, I made my way back to the town.

'We worked hard at it throughout the night,' said Yerokhimov. 'I made you a promise that I'd help you, so that you'd have something to show the inspectors when they turned up. For a long time I couldn't work out what help I could give you. Then I came up with the very thing. Want to take a look at them?'

'Look at whom?' I asked in agitated tones.

'At the priest, the police chief and the mayor,' explained Yerokhimov. 'I've got the lot locked up in the pig pen. I'll send them home after the inspectors have been. Don't think for one moment that anyone will find out. No one's allowed near the graves, and the fine fellows under my command know how to keep mum. *And now you'll have something to show the inspectors.*'

I looked at his features in profile and was reminded of Potemkin. I went to make sure that Yerokhimov was telling the truth and satisfied myself that he was. From the pig sty I could hear the bass tones of a priest singing psalms in mournful tones and adding the refrain: 'Lord have mercy; Lord have mercy.'

And then my thoughts turned to Potemkin's villages.

THERE IS A HITCH WITH THE PRISONERS

The Petersburg Cavalry Regiment proved completely unable to live down to Comrade Yerokhimov's expectations of them. Not only did they fail to desert to the enemy, but they even brought in prisoners, two Bashkir squadrons who had mutinied against their captain, Bakhivaleyev, and gone over to the side of the Red Army. The grounds for their mutiny lay in Bakhivaleyev's refusal to let them burn down a village during the course of their retreat. Now they thought they'd try their luck with the other side.

Besides the Bashkirs, the Petersburg Regiment brought in other prisoners in the form of sandal-wearing youngsters of between seventeen and nineteen. They'd been mobilised by the Whites and had been looking for the earliest opportunity to take to their heels.

There were perhaps three hundred of them, looking gaunt in what was left of their civilian clothes. There were Tartars, Mordvins and Cheremisses among them, people who understood as much about the Civil War as about solving quadratic equations.

They arrived in full military formation with rifles and cartridges, bringing with them some colonel of theirs whom they prodded into leading the march. This old Tsarist colonel, bristling with rage and eyes rolling wildly, did not let captivity prevent him from repeating to his former subordinates, even as he was led like a bear at the end of a rope, that they were swine whose snouts were in for a thrashing.

I gave orders for the billeting of the prisoners in an empty distillery and for the rations of the Petersburg Cavalry and Tver Revolutionary Regiment to be dipped into on a half-and-half basis in order to feed them.

As soon as this order had been issued, Comrade Yerokhimov and the Commander of the Petersburg Cavalry Regiment rushed up to me demanding categorically that as Commanding Officer at the Front and of the Town I should provide for the prisoners myself.

At the same time Comrade Yerokhimov made it clear that so far as the section of prisoners to be allocated to him for feeding purposes was concerned, they would be eating bullets.

For this he received a kick in the shins from the commander of the Petersburg Cavalry, who asked him to stop talking nonsense. No one was going to shoot his prisoners. That could have been done right away at the front, not now after his cavalrymen had been sharing bread and tobacco with them all this time.

If he was going to have anyone shot, it would be that Colonel Makarov of the 54th Sterlitamak Regiment.

I was opposed to this, pointing out that all officers of the old Tsarist army, even those taken prisoner, should be seen as mobilised forces covered by the Decree of June 16th, 1918.

Colonel Makarov would be sent to the military headquarters of the Eastern Front, where there were already a number of former Tsarist Officers who were actually members of the staff there.

Comrade Yerokhimov expressed the opinion that this was precisely how counter-revolution went crawling through the ranks of the Red Army. I explained to him that these people were supervised from above by political authorities and that they were used exclusively in their capacity as experts. Nevertheless, Yerokhimov was nearly in tears as he went on, full of revolutionary zeal: 'I'll never ask you for anything again, sweetheart. Just let me have that colonel.'

Menace entered his tone as he continued: 'You know perfectly well that the inspectors will be here any day now. What are you going to say to them? That a colonel fell into our hands and was allowed to leave again alive and well? To blazes with these decrees. Perhaps they were the work of experts too.'

In an instant the Commander of the Petersburg Cavalry was on his feet and yelling at Yerokhimov: 'What about that Lenin? Is he an expert? Answer me, you rogue! And the Supreme Soviet of People's Commissars, which issues these decrees, is that full of experts? What a scoundrel you are! What a cur!'

He took hold of Yerokhimov by the collar and threw him out of the room while he went on raging: 'Where was his regiment when we captured Chishma and took two squadrons of Bashkir prisoners and a battalion of the 54th Sterlitamak Regiment, its colonel included? Where was he hiding with his Tver Revolutionary Regiment? Where was he skulking with his band of villains when General Kapel's forces and the Poles were within twenty-five versts of Bugulma? I'll get hold of my cavalry and we'll drive the whole of his famous revolutionary regiment like cattle until they reach the front line. Then I'll have machine-guns positioned right behind them and make them launch an attack. Despicable wretch!' His curses took in Yerokhimov's regiment and his mother, and he only fell silent when I pointed out that the re-deployment of troops was the prerogative of the Commander of the Front alone on the basis of an order from Military Headquarters.

So he went back to the beginning of our discussion and the maintenance of prisoners, which he insisted was the responsibility of the Commander of the Front and the Commanding Officer of the town. Not so much as a single kopek would come from him. The regimental coffers ran to a total of twelve thousand roubles and his three applications to the field treasury for money hadn't produced a single rouble.

I assured him that as Commander of the Front and Commanding Officer of the town my resources amounted to two roubles. If I was to tot up everything outstanding for that month alone, owed to various organisations which had provided supplies to military units passing through the town, then the bill would come to over a million roubles. I had passed the bills on to the head quartermaster in Simbirsk and through the office of State Control, but not a single bill had been paid so far. My month's stay had yielded the following balance sheet:

Assets – 2 roubles

Liabilities – 1,000,000+ roubles.

The munificent implications of such turnover meant that for three days I had been drinking tea with milk – nothing more – and a little white bread to go with it. That was my rations for morning, noon and night. You couldn't find a single sugar lump here. Meat I hadn't had sight of for a week and so far as *shchi* was concerned, I hadn't had soup in me for more than a fortnight. As for butter or a nice piece of dripping, I couldn't even say what they looked like any more.

My tale of woe brought tears to the eyes of the Commander of the Petersburg Cavalry.

He was clearly moved. 'If things are like that, I'll take care of feeding all the prisoners myself. We've a trainful of provisions – spot of looting in the enemy's rear.' He asked me for the exact number of prisoners and left. After he'd gone I got in touch directly with Staff HQ at the Eastern Front and we exchanged telegrams, two concerning economic matters and one on the number of prisoners. The message from the Front ran as follows:

Field treasury given orders to advance you twelve million roubles. Prisoners to be conscripted into army. Place Bashkir squadrons inside Petersburg Cavalry Regiment as autonomous unit, then add other Baskkir prisoners to make First Soviet Bashkir Regiment. Place captured battalion of 54th Sterlitamak Regiment inside Tver Revolutionary Regiment. Parcel out prisoners among companies of regiment. Send Colonel Makarov to Staff HQ of Eastern Front forthwith. If unwilling, shoot instead.

I sent for Comrade Yerokhimov and for the Commanding Officer of the Petersburg Cavalry.

Only the Commander of the Petersburg Cavalry made an appearance. Instead of Yerokhimov, his regimental aide-de-camp turned up to inform me that Comrade Yerokhimov had just got hold of two armed soldiers and gone with them to fetch Colonel Makarov out of the distillery, where the prisoners were housed, and take him to the forest.

I rode after Yerokhimov and caught up with the four of them just as they were turning off the road to Little Bugulma into a spruce forest.

'Where do you think you're going?' I yelled at him. Yerokhimov had the startled look of a schoolboy caught by the teacher up his pear tree, stuffing his pockets full of fruit.

He stared helplessly for a while at the colonel, at the forest, at his soldiers and at his boots. Then came some shyly-spoken words: 'Just taking a stroll, a little stroll into the forest, with the colonel here.'

'Right,' I said. 'That's enough strolling. You go on ahead and I'll make my way back with the colonel.'

There wasn't a trace of fear to be seen in the colonel, who was bristling with fury instead. I led my horse by the bridle and the colonel made his way beside me.

'Colonel Makarov,' I said, 'I have just got you out of something very unpleasant. Tomorrow I'm sending you to our Staff HQ in Simbirsk. You'll be working for us,' I added in amiable tones.

Hardly were the words out of my mouth when the colonel struck my temple with such a blow from his bear's paw of a fist that I keeled over into the snow beside the path without so much as a squeal. In all likelihood I'd have frozen to death there, had not a couple of muzhiks heading out of Bugulma come across me a short while later. They turned round and took me home.

The following day I removed Colonel Makarov from the list of prisoners. I also took the cavalry horse, on which Colonel Makarov had made his escape from the Reds back to his Whites, off the list of horses belonging to the town's Commanding Officer. This was the very moment when Comrade Yerokhimov, who had made his way to Klyukvennoye, used the telegraph office at the railway station to send the following message to the Revolutionary Military Council of the Eastern Front at Simbirsk:

Prisoner Colonel Makarov of the 54th Sterlitamak Regiment released by Comrade Gašek and given horse for deserting to enemy.
Yerokhimov

This time the telegram got through to Simbirsk.

BEFORE THE REVOLUTIONARY TRIBUNAL OF THE EASTERN FRONT

'*....Schlechte Leute haben keine Lieder.*' I think that's how the German poet completed his couplet: There are no songs for bad people. That evening I sang Tartar songs so long into the night that no one around me could take themselves peacefully to bed, let alone sleep. I can only conclude from this that the tales of the German poet were tall ones.

Even so, I think that I was the first in the whole neighbourhood to find sleep, because I managed to tire myself with the monotonous sounds I was making, where every tune ends in an *el, el, bar, ale, ele, bar, bar, bar.*

It was one of my Chuvashes who woke me up. He told me that sledges had arrived with three people who were waving their credentials around at the guards downstairs. If you want an exact translation of his words, it would be: 'Three sledges, three people, heap papers downstairs, one, two, three papers.'

'Want speak with you,' the Chuvash went on. 'Bad people, make curses.'

'Send them up here!'

A moment later the door flew open and the visitors stormed into my office-cum-sleeping quarters.

The first was fair-haired and full-bearded, the second was a woman hidden inside a fur coat and the third was a man with a black moustache and a penetrating stare.

They had a rota for introducing themselves. 'I am Sorokin. I am Kalibanova. I am Agapov.'

The last of these added in a harsh and implacable tone: 'We are the Committee of the Revolutionary Tribunal of the Eastern Front.'

I offered them cigarettes and in return Agapov offered an observation:

'I can see that you're not badly off here, Comrade Gašek. People who serve the revolution honourably could never afford tobacco of such quality.'

When the samovar was brought in we entertained ourselves with other matters. Sorokin spoke about literature and informed us that when he'd been a left social revolutionary*, he'd published a collection of poems in Petersburg under the title *Resistance*, only to have them seized by the

*) The 'Left Social Revolutionaries' were a splinter group who left the Socialist-Revolutionary Party when the latter decided to support the Provisional Russian Government formed in February 1917. Instead

Publications Commissariat. He did not regret that nowadays, because what he'd written then had been pure tosh. He had studied modern philology and was now the President of the Revolutionary Tribunal of the Eastern Front. He was a nice man, as soft in nature as his long, fair beard, which I took to gently tweaking while we were drinking tea.

Comrade Kalibanova was a medical student and had also been a member of the Left Social Revolutionary. A lively and pleasant little person, she had conned the whole of Marx by rote. The third member of the revolutionary tribunal was the one with the most radical opinions of all. He had worked as a clerk for a Moscow lawyer who once provided sanctuary for the White General Kalenin when he was in hiding. This lawyer was, in Agapov's words, the worst villain in the world, because he paid him no more than fifteen roubles per month. This was only a third of what he gave to the waiter in the Hermitage as a tip when the man brought him a slice of salmon, asking in return merely that the man would let him spit in his face.

His whole appearance highlighted the fact that all the events preceding the fall of Tsarism had turned him into something cruel and implacable, a hard and terrible human being. He had settled accounts long beforehand with those who paid him those miserable fifteen roubles. He was a man doing battle with phantoms of the past, bathing his surroundings wherever he went in the dull glow of suspicion and making out the forms of traitors unknown.

He spoke curtly in snappish sentences full of sarcasm. When I asked him whether he might like a sugar lump in his tea, he replied: 'Life is only sweet for some, Comrade Gašek, but it will soon turn sour.'

they backed the Bolsheviks in their communist insurrection and many became zealous supporters of, and officials in, the new Soviet government.

When, in the course of our conversation, the subject of my being Czech came up, Agapov's comment was:

'However much you feed a wolf, he keeps his eyes fixed on the forest.'

Comrade Sorokin's response to this observation was to say:

'Everything will be made clear by the investigation.' Then Comrade Kalibanova said with a sneer: 'Time to show Comrade Gašek what it means to have the mandate we've been given.'

I told them that it would please me greatly to know with whom I had the honour of dealing. After all, I couldn't be expected to let anyone wake me during the night without serious cause.

At this point Agapov opened a briefcase and showed me their credentials which came in the following form:

The Revolutionary Military Council
Staff Headquarters, Eastern Front
No. 728-b
Simbirsk

A Mandate without Limitation
...is hereby conferred upon A. Sorokin, Kalibanova and Agapov. They are appointed by the Revolutionary Military Council of the Eastern Front as members of the Committee of the Revolutionary Tribunal of the Eastern Front. In this capacity they are authorised to carry out investigations wheresoever and with whomsoever they wish. We order all military units to place men at their disposal in order to carry out the sentences which they pass.

The Revolutionary Military Council
Staff HQ, Eastern Front
(Signatures Appended)

'I think that should be clear enough, Comrade Gašek,' said Kalibanova.

'No doubt,' I agreed, 'but please do remove that fur coat. The samovar will be coming in a moment and in any case it's warm in here.'

Agapov could not let the chance to intervene slip by: 'Do you feel warm? I'd say you were feeling the heat.'

'I have a thermometer here,' I explained. 'If you'd like to take a look by the window, you'll see that the temperature is normal.'

As the most serious of the three, Sorokin removed his short fur coat and put it on my bed, explaining that straight after tea we'd get down to business.

If I have cherished the memory of Comrade Agapov to this day, it is because I admired his plain talking and openness.

He was the one who asked me to have the samovar cleared away so that proceedings could begin with the main accusation against me. There was no need to summon witnesses. The charge, which had already been worked out in Simbirsk on the basis of a telegram from Comrade Yerokhimov, was quite enough in itself.

The telegram stated that I'd released Colonel Makarov and given him my horse, enabling him to go over to the enemy.

Agapov proposed that proceedings be closed and demanded that I go before a firing squad. A sentence which should be carried out within twelve hours.

I asked Comrade Sorokin who was actually the President in charge of proceedings. His answer was that everything was in perfect order, Agapov being the representative of the Prosecution.

Then I requested that Comrade Yerokhimov be summoned, because anyone can send a telegram in the first flush of anger. Let him be examined orally as a witness.

Agapov declared himself in full agreement with this. If Yerokhimov sent a telegram there was bound to be more that he knew and didn't send.

We agreed that Yerokhimov should be summoned at once to give evidence about me.

I sent for Yerokhimov....

He was tetchy and half-asleep on arrival. When Agapov informed him that what he saw before him was the Revolutionary Tribunal of the Eastern Front, which had been dispatched to make an on-the-spot inquiry into the case of Comrade Gašek and pronounce judgment, Yerokhimov's face assumed the stolid expression of those with infinite depths of mindlessness.

He looked at me. What was going on in that mind of his then is a psychological puzzle that has continued to baffle me to this very day.

He shifted his gaze from one member of the Revolutionary Tribunal to another and then finally to me.

I gave him a cigarette and said: 'Have a smoke, Comrade Yerokhimov. It's the very same good tobacco we enjoyed smoking together that other time.'

Once again Yerokhimov surveyed the whole gathering with a look as mindless as it was hopeless. Then he said: 'I sent that telegram when I was drunk as a lord, my dear comrades.'

Comrade Sorokin then rose to deliver a lecture on the evils of alcoholism. He called it the green serpent.

Then Kalibanova spoke in the same vein until Agapov got up and in a voice full of indignation demanded that Yerokhimov be punished severely for his drunkenness, because he had been Commanding Officer of the Tver Revolutionary Regiment when he committed this crime.

Resplendent in his zeal, Agapov demanded the firing squad.

I stood up and said that there wasn't a single person to be found who would shoot Yerokhimov. Such a move would provoke mutiny in the ranks.

Kalibanova proposed twenty years of forced labour. Sorokin wanted him reduced in rank.

They argued for and against each of their ideas throughout the night, until they finally fixed upon a severe reprimand for Yerokhimov and a warning that if he ever repeated his offence he would face the strictest of all sentences.

Yerokhimov himself was fast asleep throughout the entire proceedings.

In the morning it was time for the Revolutionary Tribunal of the Eastern Front to depart. When Agapov took his leave he repeated once more in a sarcastic voice:

'However much you feed a wolf, he keeps his eyes fixed on the forest. Watch how you go, bro', or you'll step on your own head.'

I gave my hand to each of them....

THE SUPREME TRUTH WHICH IS CHÊN-SHIH

I received an order to organise consciousness-raising activities for the Chinese regiment that had been sent to us in Irkutsk from the buffer region of the Eastern Siberian Republic. I immediately dashed off a few words to the regiment's Commanding Officer, one Sun-Fu:

'Please could you pop in to the army's political unit.' By way of reply I received a red envelope onto which a strip of blue paper with the address had been pasted as a sign of the highest respect.

The contents were written according to all the rules of propriety pertaining to Mandarin grammar.

Noble and Most Gracious Sir,

Yesterday I had the honour of receiving your communication, using such flattering terms of address that reading what you had written brought shame upon my head and a feeling that I was unworthy of such an honour.

By means of this poor missive I hasten to express to you, noble and most gracious Sir, my profoundest gratitude that I, of all people, may venture to enter into discussion with one such as you through a personal encounter. In now delivering to you in written form this expression of the greatest admiration and respect, pray allow me to use this unforgettable occasion to wish you the most perfect happiness.

Your most humble servant, Sun-Fu,
also Commanding Officer of the First Chinese regiment of the Irkutsk Province, former General of Chinese battalions in the Nau-Ch'in, Ling-Hu, Chêng-Ch'ieh, Hsing-Shih, Wu-Chêng and Shuang-Ling districts of the Republic of China.

I remembered that when a Chinaman writes to you like that about meeting up, he means to avoid you like the plague. Therefore I decided that it was better to send for him.

They brought me a Chinaman advanced in years and sporting a grease-stained English coat, jodhpurs and boots.

As a mark of respect he kept his slanted eyes perpetually cast down. Once we'd settled a few polite formalities together concerning which of us might be the first to take a seat, Sun-Fu, in accordance with the rules of etiquette, produced a visiting card.

On one side of the card was his name, while the other showed a family motto, inherited from his ancestors, which had been decoratively shaped into a square formation:

Hao-ming pu-ch'u-mên-o-ming-hsing-ch'ien-li
A good reputation stays put while a bad one spreads itself far and wide.

We lit cigarettes and began to chat with the aid of an interpreter. Etiquette required that Sun-Fu divulge his life story as he saw fit.

'I, Sun-Fu', he began, 'when eighteen years of age and in a state of penury, sold my house through the good offices of Hou-Ch'i to a merchant called Shih. This house, bequeathed to me by my ancestors, lay within Shim-Chih-Mên gates, behind Ch'i-Shou-Wei prison in Beijing. The house boasted sixty-eight rooms containing windows, doors, screens, wooden blinds and walls which had been there to see my ancestors before they saw me. I received twelve hundred silver taels, which sum I duly obtained from the merchant Shih through the good offices of Wang-Ts'ung and an official called T'ung-Chih, having passed over to them nine certificates confirming my ownership of the house. Then I paid a bill of exchange outstanding to the Yü-T'ai banking emporium in Sau-Têng province, amounting to something in the region of one thousand silver taels, before leaving for Shanghai. This took place exactly seven years, six moons and thirteen days into the governorship of Kauau-Ts'ui.

In Shanghai I spent twelve years studying in the military barracks of Shau-Chêu-Hêng and was appointed general. That was when I received from the government a gift of two bags of small black dried turtles, one bag of nests made from a special kind of celandine, two bags of cinnamon, one bag of dried fish and three bags of cowhide. I managed to sell the lot to the merchant Shang-Chêu-Hau, who paid me four thousand one hundred taels in pure silver and a box of opium. I had been marked out as future Commandant of the Port of Shanghai, but then misfortune struck me. At a farewell banquet for officers of the military garrison I offended Hou-Fa, a casino employee to whom all the officials owed money. As a punsihment they banished me to the northern garrisons in Nau-Chêu, Ling-Hu, Hsing-Shih, Wu-Chêng, Shuang-Ling and Chêng-Ch'ieh. Every six months I received a red certificate, also known as a pu-fa, and a lu-ch'êng-tsên, a certificate that called upon me to organise a drive to collect taxes in the name of our Most Accomplished President Yüan-Shih-K'ai, who was the embodiment of Tu-Tsa, the Money-Grubber.

All the kuan-fu, the mandarins of the Northern provinces, were afraid of me, because of the emphasis I placed upon moral rectitude, seeking chên-shih in the Northern provinces, namely the highest truth which leads to perfection. But as the saying goes, truth burns your eyes like fire. Vile enemies informed the government in the North that I was t'an-mo or, as they say in the North, t'an-tsang-ti, a man who takes bribes, even though as I have made clear I lay great store by moral rectitude and am prepared to accept only hsiao-ch'êng-ch'êng-i, small gifts to cover my travel expenses. Whereas I strove for perfection, and when on a mission even devoted myself to studying books of sages from the First Dynasties, my enemies had fallen into the hands of the basest of desires and brought a charge against me. They claimed that I provided guards for the head postmaster in the province of Hsing-Hsi, my dear and most excellent friend Yü-Chêng-Kuan, who was on his way to Peking bearing taxes and customs duties collected from the Mongolian border region. They said that I did this so that the said Yü-Chêng-Kuan could conveniently disappear without trace.

Under the Fifth Dynasty a book was once published called Mou-I-Mou, which was a primer concerning how to arouse suspicion against another person. I do not know whether a copy circulated in the Northern provinces, but it seems that one indeed did, because an unending stream of suits was laid at the door of the Supreme Court there, Nei-kê, in which I was accused of offences and wickedness of the most heinous kind, amounting to a claim that my forces were not chün-shih, that is to say regular soldiers, but chieh-lu-tuan-hsing, that is to say robbers trawled from the byways and prisons, Hun-hutzes who were hai-k'ou.

It may well be that I was not strict enough with my soldiers, because I tried to do good by each one of them, and knowing that no one is perfect I never asked them who was right and who was at fault. The intrigues of my enemies, however, reached such a level that in my last engagement, when our garrison lay in the town of Shuang-Ling, troops were sent challenging me to szŭ-hsing, which means a summons to have one's head cut off without any judicial inquiry, thereby avoiding thirty-two degrees of torture. So I blew the Shuang-Ling fortifications to smithereens and summoned my forces with the words: Ch'u-chêng ch'u-ping! Let's march across the border!

And so we marched across Mongolia, collecting gifts to cement friendship and slaughtering all those who stood in our way, showing mercy to those who treated us kindly and showed us yu-li kuan-tai, the respect shown by one brother to another, because the scholar Lao-Tse used to say that the highest and supreme perfection is brotherhood between all people. That's why I would never permit my soldiers to build pyramids out of the severed heads of their captives.'

Sun-Fu fell silent. Both he and the interpreter had been speaking at an unusually rapid tempo. If Sun-Fu had been tweeting like a bird in the Southern Chinese manner, the Korean had been singing his interpretation as perfectly as Sun-Fu had been speaking the original. It was clear that both of them were tired, but even so Sun-Fu was marshalling his thoughts on how to account for his reaching the buffer zone of the Eastern Siberian Republic and from there getting to Irkutsk.

Finally Sun-Fu bowed to the interpreter and to myself before continuing: 'We arrived from the sandy wilderness of Hang-Au, where instead of sheep we came upon nothing but yen-ch'ên-t'u, mountains of dust. To the North of us was Urga and in a southerly direction, where the sun turns towards the West, lay Hsi-tsang, Tibet and, in a westerly direction, O-Kuo, Russia. We headed in a westerly direction, West and nothing but West, until we reached Russia, somewhere between Buryat and the Selenge region, on the River Selenge, a place called Jun-Dar, a valley through which you can get to Shang-T'ou-Tu-I-Skin, also known as Upper Udinsk. It is there that Ch'ao-T'ung-Shêng, governor of the province, received our forces. However, my enemies continued their pursuit even to this place, and so we were sent as far as Baikal in O-Kuo, Russia.

'Today I can see that a lot of people fall short of perfection in so many ways, and that if I am not spotless myself there are others still further from the way that seeks the impeccable by letting a moral purpose permeate all that they do. This is what I have striven for my whole life through, seeking redemption through the knowledge of truth.'

He fell silent again and his slanted eyes began to wander from one object to another until finally they fixed themselves upon me with a cold look of utter indifference. It was as if he wanted to say: 'Ch'üan-tsa-pai, white devil, you are nothing to me.'

My response to Sun-Fu through the interpreter went as follows:

'I am most obliged to you for that brief life story, which tells us all about your perfection. It's crystal clear to me that your regiment, being no less perfect than you are, needs only fa-kuang-chiao-hua – I might call this a consciousness-raising committee. School visits, theatre performanes, lectures – that sort of thing. No regiment should be without them. Bring me a proposal by the day after tomorrow. Whatever you think suits the needs of your countrymen.'

Sun-Fu replied through the interpreter:

'Culture is closely connected to education and morality in all their forms. Chiao-hua, culture, tries to grasp what is true. It cannot be kept in check or be subject to error, but must proceed from the heart and from ethics and be based on ch'uan-ts'o, the follies of the human condition. I am delighted to have the opportunity to present you with my proposals in the area you mention on the day after tomorrow. I feel, however, that these ideas of mine will be too tsui-o, that is to say of such little value and of so base a nature, that it fills me with shame to think of having received such an offer from you. Your offer is so appreciative of my talents that I feel too obliged to refuse to carry out what I yet know to be of such little worth.'

Sun-Fu rose to his feet and proferred me a hand which was as cold to the touch as his eyes. The interpreter, a Korean, removed his glasses as a mark of respect when he gave me his own hand.

They went out leaving behind them the scent of garlic and beaver fat which is the spirit of China and always makes it necessary to air the room.

It had slipped my mind that the previous day a military commissar from the Fifth Army had said to me in the course of a conversation concerning Sun-Fu: 'The man's a scoundrel.'

As evening drew on, a second Chinaman turned up to visit me. He was a small man in black clothes and with not a single hair on his head. His face had the pale gold sheen of a connoisseur of the opium pipe. Clean shaven under the nose, his chin was the one place where a thinly spread band of black hairs was to be seen. There was something humorous about this face, but it was difficult to make out whether it betokened a smile or a grimace of some kind

The Chinese have an unusually elaborate rumour mill. If two of them meet, you can be sure that they will say concerning a third: 'I've just seen Po-Ch'ia-Tsa buying vegetables from Shêng-Shêng.' And the other will certainly say in reply: 'And took them straight to the home of Jên-Chu-Jên.'

So it came as no surprise to me that my guest began:

'Sem-Fu been here, Colonel Sun-Fu been here, me Lu-J-Jao, me speaking Russian, me no need interpreter, me know Russian wall (he meant 'well'). Sun-Fu, he colonel, been here. Sun-Fu, colonel, no godly, no godly.'* I offered him tea and cigarettes, and in response Lu-J-Jao grimaced pleasantly. Then he went on talking, inserting many Chinese words from a northern dialect into his speech, making our discussion even more difficult and beyond hope of comprehension.

'I Lu-J-Jao, never been sha-tai, idiots. Me hang-shih-chang-liao, me mai-mai-hsing-ch'i-lai-liao.'

I tried to stem the tide and explain to him that an interpreter had to be present, whereupon he rejoined:

'She stands on own feet, she breathing, breathing, no fall down.'

This strange sentence was a literal, and therefore of course bad, translation of a lengthy Chinese expression which meant something like: 'In that case I'm off.'

However, he remained seated and it became clear to me that there was nothing he wished for more than to have an interpreter present. It was just that Lu-J-Jao felt that by refusing one he was simply being polite by saving me bother.

*) It is very hard to convey in Czech just how bad Lu-J-Jao's Russian was. His 'Me' meant 'I'. Chinese has no gender, no case, and not even a hint of declension or conjugation. In spite of this they go ahead and transform their words into other languages. The 'no godly no godly' is the Russian word 'negodyai' (scoundrel, ne'er-do-well). [Author's note]

I made a call on the intercom and began speaking to the office, asking them to send the interpreter Li-P'i-T'i.

A few words told me that Lu-J-Jao was well acquainted with the fact that the interpreter was Korean, a member of a nation that, when it knows a thing or two about someone Chinese, takes great pleasure in failing to divulge its information to anyone else who's Chinese.

Thanks to Li-P'i-T'i I soon found out the reason for my visitor's arrival.

Lu-J-Jao set the ball rolling as follows:

'I, Lu-J-Jao, have come here to warn you about Sun-Fu. He is a man who can only be described as hsiao-chang, that is to say unworthy to be ground under the soles of my feet. You don't know who Lu-J-Jao is. In the twenty-second province of China they know who I am. Do you know what Ch'iu-wên-pu-ya-ya-yü-jên is? You mean you don't know the magazine *Let No One Use their Erudition to Confound Others?* What about *The Brotherhood of Hearts at One*? That journal used to be produced in Szŭ-ch'uan. Don't you know that I, Lu-J-Jao, am the editor of these publications? Yes, I, Lu-J-Jao, I am he, and he knows Sun-Fu all too well. How did Sun-Fu conduct himself in the province of Kuang-Tung, in Chê-Chiang, or in Kuang-Hsi? Why were they hunting him down bearing arrest warrants in the ports of Hsi-Mao, Meng-Tzŭ and Su-Chou? Why did he have to escape from prison in Ch'êng-Tu and Fu-Chou, not to mention Yün-Nan and Shan-Tung? Why was he lying low in Korea for three years, in Chemulpo, Fusan, Kunzanpo and Yuaushan. The man's a 'General'? Not likely! I would now like you to prick up your ears. Sun-Fu is hsiung-šou, a brigand, an assassin. I do not wish to upset you with this news, because with a pure heart I wish you all the very best, though even I can fall victim to an imperfection or two. I am, however, a lover of truth, of chên-shih, the highest truth which aims at perfection. That is why I am so well-liked here. I would be only too happy if you would always, when you wish to be informed about something concerning any of my compatriots, turn to me and to me alone. You will always see the truth of my words, for such am I, the ever-truthful Lu-J-Jao, much loved by his compatriots.'

After a lengthy period during which I thanked him for the information he had given me, assured him that he would always be the one I would turn to and asked him to leave me his address, Lu-J-Jao's eyes took on a similarly cold expression to those of Sun-Fu. It was as if he too wanted to say: 'Ch'üan-tsa-pai, you are nothing to me, white devil!'

The following morning I was informed that two more Chinamen wanted to speak with me. When they were ushered in, I could see at a glance that I had the honour of speaking to Chinamen faultlessly attired in the European manner, with elegant American-style shoes. The older one even wore gloves. Both spoke French with ease and the older introduced himself as follows : 'Tsung-Li-Ya-Mên, Chinese consul in Irkutsk. Allow me to present my secretary, Ku-Chiao-Chang.' He proceeded to speak for half an hour, explaining the reasons for his visit: in the first place he wished to introduce himself and put himself at my disposal should I be in need of anything (a rather puzzling offer, wouldn't you say?) In the second place he gathered that a certain Lu-J-Jao had paid me a visit the previous evening. He had come to warn me about this person. The ways of his compatriots were still unfamiliar to me and so I must rely on his word and understand that Lu-J-Jao was the biggest scoundrel the world had seen. He was peerless in the villainy stakes. He ran a network of Hun-hutze people and smugglers in Charbin. He had killed several Russian merchants. Yes, that's what Lu-J-Jao was like, last heard of preying upon the Chinese, supplying them with some resin in lieu of opium. Lu-J-Jao's tentacles also spread deep inside Russia, and when he affected to speak the language badly it was mere trickery. During the Russo-Japanese war he had been a spy as well as an interpreter for the Japanese. Some years ago he had swindled money out of a rich Chinese merchant in Moscow, who paid him to transport the body of his late wife to China. Instead he took the coffin to Odessa and had her interred in a cemetery there. The rest of the money which had been paid for her to be taken to China he pocketed for himself, using it to set up a gambling joint in the port, raking in the losses of many visitors. Here in Irkutsk he was now scheming against Tsung-Li-Ya-Mên himself, writing to the Revolutionary Committee denouncing the Chinese consul for smuggling Chinese people with gold to China. Lu-J-Jao was detested by all Chinese people and generally avoided by them.

The Chinese consul's secretary, the aforementioned Ku-Chiao-Chang, added the remark that Lu-J-Jao traded his wife to a Burjat nomad for a wretched nag that he rode around on when being pursued through the Chitinskaya region for robbery and multiple murders.

I asked these gentlemen what they made of Colonel Sun-Fu.

'Splendid fellow,' replied the Chinese consul, 'Beyond reproach in every way. Upright and truthful, this is a man heading at full speed for that state of perfection which is revealed in the sacred teachings of Lao-Kur.'

'A most agreeable fellow,' added the consul's secretary, 'the best and most honourable person that I have ever met.'

Tsung-Li-Ya-Mên then took his leave of me with the words: 'Rest assured that should you ever want information about anyone, I am at your service. I know all there is to know about the local Chinese community. They are all beholden to me. In fact there is never a time when they don't need me. I am their father and mother in one.'

After their departure some Chinaman brought me a painted cabinet decorated in the familiar Chinese way. There was the usual bird among reeds, for instance. Inside the cabinet were sweets made from cane sugar which gave off an unpleasant odour of musk. There was a note above the sweets written on red paper and with unusually polite contents, which were disclosed to me by the interpreter Li-P'i-T'i:

Most Esteemed Sir,

It was the greatest pleasure to learn that you were residing in this town, which makes such a sweet and indelible impression on me in the light of your arrival, for your presence illuminates every street of the said small city. Forgive the presumption of my wishing to realise what would be the greatest honour of my life, namely the chance to speak with you in person. I await your decision on this matter, for my fate is in your hands. Be your decision what it may, your answer will always be treasured like the rarest gem. Please excuse my impertinence and allow me to wish you complete and perfect happiness.

Huang-Hun

'Don't believe anything a Chinaman says,' the Korean interpreter told me when I dictated my reply to the note, saying that I would be delighted to have the honour of meeting Mr Huang-Hun in person.

'These Chinese,' the Korean informed me on his way out, 'are tai-tsai-ti-chu, or suporosnaya svinya—pregnant pigs' as the Russians say.'

When I asked Mr Huang-Hun, who was quite good at Russian, why he wrote to me in Chinese, he explained that it was a question of good manners, because he thought that I might like such notes for my collection. When he was working in the tea business in Moscow some years ago, he used to sell his business letters to collectors.

However, that was not the reason why he had come. His visit had one purpose only, which was to warn me about the successful exploits of a couple of well-known rogues, namely one Tsung-Li-Ya-Mên, who was masquerading as the Chinese consul, and one Ku-Chiao-Chang, who was pretending to be his secretary. Mr Huang-Hun offered to make things clearer by reminding me that when Irkutsk was still being governed by Admiral Kolchak there were a couple of villains who made several millions out of misappropriating supplies of rice supposedly destined for the army. They were sentenced to the Cheremkov coal mines. After the coup d'état they escaped from the mines and arrived in Irkutsk at just the moment when the Chinese consul, mindful of the extremely preferential treatment he had provided to the now deceased Admiral, decided to flee the place. The two immediately announced their acceptance of the post of consul, had their official seals made and everything went ahead.

'And what do you make of Lu-J-Jao?' I asked Mr Huang-Hun.

'A paragon,' came the reply, 'Man of honour, forthright fellow. Striving for truth, on the path to perfection.'

Huang-Hun took his leave of me in the most cordial manner, having inquired as to whether he might send me some real tea from the South of China.

Once he'd gone I must confess that my head was in a spin. Where was this highest truth that led to perfection as the Buddha wished, this chên-shih, to be found?

The next few days saw my head in even more of a tizzy. In the first place some T'ou-Mu turned up and accused Mr Huang-Hun of forging banknotes and other crimes.

Mr Hsiung-Chien informed me that Sun-Fu was a scoundrel, while the Chinese consul and his secretary were the most upstanding fellows under the sun. Mr Lao-P'o-Tsa made it clear that T'ou-Mu, Huang-Hun, the Chinese consul plus secretary, Lu-J-Jao and even Mr Hsiung-Chien were rotten to the core, the unworthiest creatures to have walked the earth in any age. There was one honourable exception to this band of rascals, and that was Colonel Sun-Fu, perfect in every way, apostle of truth and one whose whole existence was without blemish.

Mr Fa-Tsa portrayed Mr Lao-P'o-Tsa in a very unfavourable light, spending a quarter of an hour listing his crimes.

Mr Lao-Ping accused Fa-Tsa of murdering his own parents and a number of lesser offences.

New revelations flowed in on a daily basis....

Colonel Sun-Fu received two thousand army coats, full uniforms and pairs of boots for his regiment from the Commissariat. He stored them in a warehouse in Inokentev Street.

Two days later he came with an interpreter to make a speech to me: 'I am delighted to see you again, although I stand before you as one who is shêng-ling, a being whose tears and grief know no limits. I bring no proposals concerning the fa-chan-chiao-hua, the raising of the consciousness of my regiment. My heart weeps and my eyelashes are glum with remorse. There has been a disaster and all is woe, all is hê-chuan, the greatest misfortune, a curse is upon us, we are tsai-nan. Villains have broken into my warehouse in Inokenstev Street and the wretched devils have made off with two thousand army coats, two thousand full uniforms and pairs of boots. A curse upon the scoundrels!'

To signal his grief Colonel Sun-Fu started to howl: 'k'u, t'i-k'u, k'u-shêng, k'u-k'u-t'i-k'u'.

I had him taken away to the main guardhouse for questioning. The interrogation made it clear that Colonel Sun-Fu set up a joint venture that plundered the warehouse containing the regiment's equipment. The list of its associates included everyone that had previously been to see me – even Lu-J-Jao and Messrs. Huang-Hun, T'ou-Mu, Hsiung-Chien, Lao-P'o-Tsa, Fa-Tsa, not to mention Lao-Ping.

The Chinese consul and his secretary, that perfect pair Tsung-Li-Ya-Mên and Ku-Chiao-Chang, had made their car available for the robbery and contented themselves with two hundred and fifty full uniforms, a bounty which was tracked down in their own warehouse.

It is said that they all made unusually fine speeches in court, interweaving their words with the reflections of ancient philosophers from ancient China, emphasising that throughout their lives they had attached supreme importance to moral standards in their behaviour, always searching for that chên-shih, that highest truth which chases after perfection.

That they happened to be looking for such truth in a warehouse in Inokentev Street housing military uniforms was simply a stroke of fate.

Chên-shih, that highest truth, cannot be brought down by a mere two thousand military uniforms and two thousand pairs of boots....

CROSS PURPOSES

The dispatch from the Siberian Revolutionary Committee in Omsk required my immediate departure from Irkutsk to Urga in Mongolia. There I would greet General Sun-Fu, a representative of the Republic of China, and negotiate everything relating to the renewal of trade relations between the Republic of China and Eastern Siberia.

The next day saw another telegram arrive. This one told me to deliver General Sun-Fu to Irkutsk so that a representative of the People's Commissariat for Foreign Affairs, one Comrade Gabranov, could discuss the treaty setting out the borders between Soviet Russia, Mongolia and China with him.

And so it came about that I set off taking with me two infantry battalions and a cavalary squadron as a guard of honour for my travels. Just so that I could be prepared for any eventuality, a battery of light artillery came along too.

From Irkutsk we made our way in formation on foot, nowhere encountering any resistance. Wherever we went we were received by Buryats bearing roast mutton and mare's milk.

We made our way without let or hindrance as far into Mongolia as the Selenge aimag. Unidentified rabble-rousers had incited the Buryats in several parts of the area around Lake Baikal, by spreading stories that I was going to commandeer their cattle.

On the steppe by Sudja we had our first encounter with armed Buryat horsemen, and when we reached Lake Ar-Meda we found ourselves up against insurgents. Three thousand of them. They sent an envoy to us with a tempting offer. We should surrender to them, and then when we'd joined forces we'd set out for the Altai mountain range where we would all eke out a living till winter as bandits. They might let us start heading home when the cold season arrived.

I turned the offer down and made my own proposal to the rebels: they should surrender to us and join our campaign instead. This would be a nice diplomatic manoeuvre, since the presence of Buryat riders among our forces could save us from attacks from the locals, who were also Buryats.

I have to admit that the ploy did not succeed in the manner I'd expected. The rebels went over to our side, it's true, but because they'd heard we had artillery weapons. And so our noble ranks were gradually swollen by three thousand wild Buryat horsemen.

Fellow-feeling among compatriots led to a further swelling of the ranks. We started to acquire nomads from the Barkugin, Mesegel and Tamir regions. By the time I was within three hundred versts of the Mongolian border we had about twelve thousand men.

In Kale-Yzyr, a little town in the steppes, a band of robbers under the Buryat overlord Ló-Tum came over to our side – perhaps eight hundred in all. Below Mount Mane-Omi we acquired a posse of Hun-hutzes about six hundred strong and so our numbers were boosted considerably, bringing us to about twenty thousand by the time we reached the Mongolian border. The local populace took off in fear when they saw us, setting up warning fires which burned through the night on the mountains. We had enormous herds of cattle by now, not to mention sheep, goats and horses, collected with great care by my cavalcade of honour wherever we went.

When we reached We-Rama, provincial capital of the Pej-Húr region of Mongolia, representatives of the Mongolian government visited us accompanied by Lamas (Buddhist priests) and implored us to let them escape with their lives. We could do what we liked with Mongolia, they explained, and they had no objection to whatever government we wished to install. It took me a long time to explain to them that I came as a friend and that my intentions were entirely peaceful. I was there for a meeting in Urga with a Chinese general named Sun-Fu.

They were quite frankly astonished by this explanation and provided me with another cavalcade of honour, this time composed of two regiments of Mongolian soldiers. As a result I finally found myself approaching Urga with thirty thousand men. The Chinese government was most taken aback and started to concentrate their forces on the Mongolian border.

The representative of the Japanese government in Peking felt insulted by such behaviour on the part of China, because even Japan had interests to defend in Mongolia.

The result was a series of sharp exchanges by telegram between Tokyo and Peking.

While all this was going on I made my quiet way to Urga in order to greet General Sun-Fu. Meanwhile he, in a state of some anxiety, began despatching forces over the Chinese border towards Urga. In the end he had threee divisions of Chinese infantry ranged against me, plus a Japanese cavalry regiment and two artillery divisions.

And so it came to mortal combat below Urga, in a battle that raged for two days. The bones of all my Buryats found their final resting-place there.

My forces were smashed to smithereens. The Urga region fell to China together with the entire Mongolian province of Pej-Húr. I made my way back to Irkutsk with just two men, and when Comrade Gabranov, the representative of the People's Commissariat for Foreign Affairs, asked me what I'd done with General Sun-Fu, I told him:

'A case of cross purposes. He stayed behind in Urga....'

SHAKE THE DUST FROM YOUR SHOES

'And if any place will not receive you and they will not listen to you, when you leave, shake off the dust that is on your feet as a testimony against them'.
(Mark 6 :11)

I It was the 4th of December, 1,850 years after the fall of Jerusalem, 428 after the discovery of America and, if that's not enough for you, 540 years after the invention of gunpowder. This was the date of my departure from Soviet Russia and arrival at the border of the Republic of Estonia.

In the city of Narva a faded poster attracted my attention; a year earlier the Estonian Government had promised a reward of 50,000 Estonian marks to persons unknown. All they had to do was catch me and string me up. This was the time when I was publishing a magazine in the Tartar-Bashkir language close to Jamburg. The target audience was a couple of divisions of savage Bashkirs and other assorted cut-throats, who were together taking on the White forces of the Republic of Estonia. The Estonians had crossed over into Russia with English support, inviting a thrashing for themselves.

50,000 Estonian marks! You have to take into account the rotten exchange rate, since you only got one German mark for 10 Estonian ones, but an attractive proposition all the same, especially for someone like me who needed money, having lost his last million Soviet roubles on the way from Moscow to Narva.

By good fortune I recalled the fact that even if I really hanged myself in Narva in order to secure the reward, nobody would believe that it was me. I was travelling under a false name and my documents were all forged.

The only thing they contained that wasn't false was my photograph.

My thoughts were interrupted by a well-dressed man who asked me in broken Russian whether I might like to exchange some Soviet roubles for Estonian marks.

I recognised him at first glance. Here I was again after many years, face to face with a plainclothes policeman. I'd already seen a long line of frontier police and guards positioned along the wire border fence. I'd looked at this arrangement in a one-sided way which I hope everyone will understand. All of Estonia had been swaddled in wire so that not a single socialist idea could make its way in.

The undercover policeman had some more to say. He was trying to entice something out of me, an unknown foreigner. He was talking about Estonia being in a shambles and was praising Soviet Russia.

Fortunately I'd learned what to say about Russia from an edition of the *National Political Review* which had been handed out to Czechs leaving the country by people working at the Czech mission run by Captain Skala in Moscow.

I told him to refrain from heaping such praise upon the Soviets, remembering something I'd read in the *Review*. I said that apparently the wife of a Czech shoemaker in St. Petersburg had been driven mad by hunger and the death of her grandfather in the village of Chrášťovice in the Beroun region of Bohemia. I also said that there were corpses on every street corner. Out of half a million Petersburgers there was just one who was still alive, and that was Mr Zinoviev, who looted the shops of what was now a ghost town in broad daylight. But all this was small beer. There were worse things. New-born babies were being....

Mr Detective did not even bid me farewell. Instead he beat a hasty retreat to the other side of the station.

I attached myself to a detachment returning from Russia in the tattered grey uniforms of old Austria, bearing rucksacks that had faded during their six years of service and talking in a medley of voices and languages representing the different nations of the former monarchy.

In a quiet corner of a small house at the station, under the sign saying 'Gents', a Hungarian captain was sewing pips onto a grease-stained collar.

In front of the castle and the old fortifications a representative of the Red Cross welcomes in German all 'severely tested' defenders of the fatherland.

From a German nurse working for the Red Cross we receive our first cup of German coffee with artificial sweetener.

The signs on the gate leading to the quarantine camp in the old castle are in German and Hungarian alone.

National flags from all but the Slavic lands are everywhere. Members of an American Association for Young

Christian Men are handing out Bibles while running a sideline in the exchange of Romanov, Kerensky and even Soviet roubles for Estonian marks. Everyone curses Russia, while Estonian soldiers secretly flog the hard stuff to those leaving the country.

The gate of the old castle once belonging to German crusaders has been closed to shut us in. We will be here for four days and no one is allowed into the town.

In the great courtyard a sorting of nations takes place. Some man shouts in German: 'Hungarian nationals to the left, Austrians to the right, Czechs in the middle and Romanians by the gates!' Turmoil breaks out at his words. By the office some former cadet is standing in tears. Someone working for the Red Cross urges him to say where he comes from.

They take him to the office and put him in front of a map. They look for Kolozsvar there and in the end he works out what has become of him. On the basis of the Peace of Versailles he has turned into a Romanian national.

The cadet weeps more tears than ever now and a Red Cross nurse gives him a sugar cube doused in valerian.

II The quarantine camp and the offices of the Red Cross are to be found within the spacious grounds of the old castle in Narva, built by German crusaders and used at one time to ravage Baltic regions with fire and sword.

Now it is the turn of English corporations to ravage them, furnishing them with unwanted pieces of artillery, fake porcelain eggs to motivate their hens to lay, electric tea-urns and sports equipment, all of them very important seeing that the Estonians themselves have nothing to eat.

The castle in Narva lies in ruins. It was destroyed several times over by the Swedes as part of their efforts to drive the German knights out of Narva. Then it was ruined all over again by Peter the Great when he was driving out the Swedes (no further details are available in any encyclopaedia). During the Civil War the walls of the castle enjoyed shellfire from both the Red side and the White.

To cap it all the Red Cross has come to complete the work of destruction. Without sparing their hoes, they proceed to turn the remains of the old Knights' Hall into unflushable toilets for former prisoners-of-war returning from Russia.

Their hoes have even been at work turning the castle turrets into storerooms which it would be worth (perish the thought) having someone inspect.

The local entrepreneurs, the profiteering part of the population, have been drilling numerous holes in the castle wall through which they sneak inside bearing their evil-smelling salamis.

Seeing that the local citizens are strictly forbidden to associate with those returning from Russia, Estonian soldiers are posted at every hole where they stand guard like cats ready to pounce on mice. The local garrison receives a constant income stream, receiving fifty per cent of every pound of salami sold and a half of all the other goods whose quality is just as lousy.

An air of designer squalor hangs over the whole castle. It gives the impression of being under siege as in olden times, when their enemies hurled stinking pots into the attack. The fragments of broken pot used to be carefully picked up by the defenders so that they would not cut through people's sandals, but the contents of the pots were lying around wherever you looked.

The buildings belonging to the former Russian barracks in the courtyard, now being used to accommodate those returning from that country, are about as pleasant to live in as the buildings which were once under siege.

Soiled plank beds, stinking stoves and the air heavy with the smell of bean soup. Wives of returning men hang the nappies of their offspring out to dry.

Let us rather take a look at the *Soldatenheim* (Soldiers' Home). The Red Cross, beneficiary of so much American money, has received a purely German makeover here and gives the impression of being a profit-making enterprise.

The nurses offer salami and coffee for sale. The coffee comes from a tin and is supposed to be distributed free to returning soldiers. They buy their salami for five marks and sell it for 25 Estonian marks or for 125 Romanov roubles or for 320 Kerensky roubles or for 1,000 Soviet roubles. To a man from the Tyrol on his way home today it is much of a muchness. He savours the aroma of German coffee and a sign saying 'Behut euch Gott' (God bless you).

The Tyrolean is moved. 'Most merciful Madam,' he says full of emotion, while he squirrels away in his pocket the salami on which he's used up his last roubles,

'I am so grateful for all the help you have given us.'

In the *Soldatenheim* all the magazines are in German. I was trying to take a look at an article in one magazine called *Freiheit* (Freedom), all about the recent lock-outs of workers in the German 'socialist republic', when there was a terrible commotion and someone outside shouted that a Hungarian had jumped off the tower into the castle moat.

I went to take a look and discovered that Captain Haranyi, formerly of the 18th Homeland Defence Unit, had jumped into the moat as a result of unsuccessful financial dealings.

It's a sorry tale of currency speculation.

Captain Haranyi was dispatched as an invalid to Moscow from the POW camp at Krasnojarsk. Once there he went to the Sukharev market in Moscow and sold his trousers for 120,000 roubles and his tunic for 80,000. So he ended up with 200,000 Soviet roubles.

Because he heard that they were not accepting Soviet roubles abroad and would offer nothing in exchange for them, he snapped up some Romanov roubles, in the form of imperial ten and fifty-rouble notes, from currency traders in Sukharev, who offered him 1,000 imperial roubles for 50,000 Soviet ones. So he ended up with 4,000 Romanov roubles. Then someone informed him that Wrangel, the commanding officer of the White army, had been trounced. So they weren't accepting Romanov roubles abroad any more. Now it was Kerensky roubles that were worth something. So he changed his 4,000 imperial roubles for 2,000 Kerensky roubles, which he found to his amazement would land him with only 400 Estonian marks in Narva. He tried to change them into German marks and was given 80. This was the last straw. He began buying up Soviet roubles again, which were being offered at a rate of 10 German marks for 1,000 Soviet roubles. That got him 8,000 roubles, which in desperation, following a fall in the value of the rouble, he changed back again into 40 marks. On Tuesday he tried some more currency speculation, this time with imperial roubles, and on Wednesday threw himself from the highest tower into the castle moat with a single Estonian mark on him, crying out: 'Eljen a Magyarország!'

They buried him behind the castle walls, a location which was also the last resting-place of 400 Russian Red Army soldiers, who were captured by the Estonians and machine-gunned to death on an embankment.

Tomorrow we're off to Tallinn.

III Getting from Narva to Tallinn is easier said than done. The whole process has to be taken in stages. To begin with, you have to strip naked and sacrifice your clothes and boots to be disinfected by a contraption that treats them to scorching heat. If you happen to be unlucky and no one explains to you that the apparatus will destroy leather items like boots and wallets, then you will find yourself confronted by a grisly horror scene.

One poor fellow handed over his boots and a wallet full of Romanov five hundred-rouble notes. He had preyed upon Russia for two years in order to amass a sufficient amount of capital and now it had all been taken away by the baking machine and turned into an unbreakable twisted lump of boiled leather containing banknotes which had returned to their primaeval state as shrivelled paper purée.

So far as the boots themselves were concerned, it was impossible to fathom the nature of the objects returned by the oven of disinfection. Two mysterious knots made up of some kind of congealed leather paste lay there in front of the unfortunate man, who was holding in one hand something that a quarter of an hour earlier could have been called a wallet filled with a fortune. All he could manage now was an idiotic stare directed at what used to be his boots.

In the end they led the unlucky fellow away barefoot to the office of the Red Cross, where they handed over a grant of fifty German marks and a coarse pair of boots, the receipt of which he was required to confirm with his signature about fifteen times over.

Throughout this unfortunate incident a different group of returnees were washing themselves in dirty, cold water, while the supervisors were laying into some brash fellows from the Hungarian part of the former Austria-Hungary, who had the temerity to steal the green soap from the bath tubs.

Finally everyone lines up, washed and disinfected, at the offices of the Red Cross, where they encounter the next procedural hurdle. An Estonian official is in charge of a list detailing who is to proceed to Tallinn in the evening. Hungarian, Romanian and Czech names are landing him with an insoluble puzzle where pronunciation is concerned.

Countless misunderstandings arise. A cry goes up for one 'Yesef Nefech!' They go in search of him. No one responds to the call. They look for him among the Turks and Romanians, while it occurs to no one that this is Josef Novák, who's been waiting among a group of Czechs so that he can take pride in shouting out in German in the castle courtyard of Narva: 'Here I am!'

It may be that Josef Novák is still in Narva to this very day waiting for them to call out his name.

A new act in the drama is about to begin, the battle of the tins, which they distribute on the basis of one box for every two men. There is no system behind what happens, and the spirit of selflessness lies in ruins weeping bitterly. They look in vain for a man who took a box to be shared with another man who stands tinless before them now. In despair the latter returns to the tail of the queue in the hope that he might succeed in getting a whole box which he will then take his turn to vanish with. In the end the storehouse is closed and the poor storekeeper has to take his pencil out and together with the dispatching agent solve the following difficult mathematical problem in his alcove:

Today 726 returnees left. On a one-box-per-two-people basis that means 363 boxes. Actual number distributed: 516.

(I warmly recommend this new dimension in arithmetical studies to the *Czech Journal of Mathematics* and to our Minister of Finance).

The same sort of thing is happening with gifts from the American Red Cross. An attractive young lady is dealing with the verbal requests of petitioners who have quickly got rid of their shirts in the barracks and now offer their bare chests as silent witnesses to their shirtless condition.

One of the claimants tries to make clear to the young lady that he's without any long johns either...

At six in the evening they finally organise us into columns of six, closely marshalled by Estonian soldiers who usher us through the gates of an orchard onto a bridge where they count us all over again.

There is an unusual measure of fluidity about our numbers. I said earlier that there were 726 of us. In the courtyard we numbered 713, at the orchard gates we'd reached 738 and now we'd climbed to 742.

An Estonian official waves a despairing hand and moans: 'Ilvaja!' which matches Russia's own expression of boundless despair: 'nichevo'.

They drive us over the bridge and then another two kilometres through the town, whose face has been left clearly scarred by the civil war.

A long line of uncovered trenches extends across the square as a reminder to later generations but also for use as a drainage system, which is currently at the same stage of evolution here as it was when the German crusaders built the town centuries ago.

On the corner of Avenue Maja I witnessed a pleasing scene. A police officer was trying to come between a hefty pig and a stray bearded goat who were tussling with one another.

That accounts for everything I saw in Narva and I can finish with the words I used to round off Part II of this sketch: 'Tomorrow we are off to Tallinn.' I give my word to readers and editor alike, that tomorrow we really will – finally – leave for Tallinn.

IV It actually took us two days to cover the 180 kilometres between Narva and Tallinn. Estonian officialdom bore down upon us with inspections at several stops. They didn't allow anyone off the train at stations and they didn't let us buy anything. Confined to the train it was like living inside a volcano. The convoy was sitting around little green stoves from which the heat had disappeared long ago on the first day of travel, because all we had for this two-day voyage was a few lumps of peat briquette. People railed against everything Estonian and even against the representative of the Red Cross.

Our longest wait was at the Estonian town of Igóratis, where open mutiny broke out in the three rear waggons of the train where the Hungarians and Romanians were situated. They surrounded the unfortunate representative of the Red Cross and angrily demanded bread from him, threatening him with a beating. This set the scene for my becoming more closely acquainted with another gentleman, an engineer by the name of Jožka. Until this moment he had remained unnoticed and unrecognised among the Germans from Austria in waggon number 7.

Nobody could have appreciated that this modest gentleman, who hailed from a POW camp containing officers captured in Semipalatinsk, was a hare-brained idealist. He placed himself between the angry crowd and the besieged Red Cross worker and in a sermonising tone of voice began:

'Now then, Gentlemen, come to your senses. I am surprised at you, yelling like that. Pray bear in mind the fact that we are on foreign soil as guests of Estonia, and that every disturbance of this sort reduces our standing in the eyes of Estonians.'

'All we're asking for,' the Romanians shouted, 'is for them to give us bread right now.' 'In Narva,' some Hungarians added very loudly, 'they gave everyone bread for half a day, so we've already been starving for 36 hours. Let's get him!'

'Bear with me, Gentlemen,' said the engineer in a tone designed to mollify, 'do not resort to force. Let the Estonians see that we know how to behave with dignity. Consider the children of this country seeing this on their way from school. What would they think?'

A half-baked idea goes around that the engineer has his own finger in the pie. Out of the crowd comes a shameless voice claiming that the man has enough bread in his own waggon to use it in the stove instead of coal. The representative of the Red Cross uses the storm about to break over the head of the engineer as an opportunity to make himself scarce. There had to be a way of relieving the tension. Two Estonian soldiers look quietly on while the engineer is given a hiding, and when it is all over they watch him straining as he crawls back into his waggon.

'What a mauling that was,' he remarked when he'd finally got inside, 'it pains me that such a thing should happen abroad in full view of foreigners. Still, it's a good thing that there were no children returning home from school to see what savages we are.'

The engineer has sacrificed himself for the representative of the Red Cross, whose conscience has reached as far as trying to persuade Estonian officials to do something for the returning convoy, even if it is only to boil up some soup for them.

His powers of persuasion seemed to bear fruit. The words about soup were hardly out of his mouth before the whole telephone system sprang to life. An order went through to the station authorising our immediate departure and the representative of the Red Cross received a promise that there would be soup for us in Igwa.

So off we go to Igwa, where we discover that there is no soup for us because we'll be receiving a whole lunch at the station in Mörigölje. In Mörigölje they hasten to get rid of us with the assurance that at Wejnemäje lunch and dinner will both be waiting for us.

To give my fellow travellers due credit, I must say that the man who brought us this information in Mörigölje had to be taken to the hospital while we moved on. At Wejnamäje we don't even stop at the station and so if there was anyone among us who might think that this man in Mörigölje was being done a wrong he was now able to change his mind completely.

It is night-time when the train draws into Tallinn. By now the people inside it are ready to do anything. In fact they are in such a mood that looting the town seems more than likely.

By the time dawn was approaching there wasn't one of us that didn't look like a hardened old lag with a lifetime of crime behind him. Our gentleman engineer is the only one who still oozes hope, supposing in his optimistic way that they really will give us food in Tallinn.

He never stops talking, and he never says anything that we haven't already known for a very long time.

'It's really so very strange,' he says, 'that when a fellow hasn't eaten for thirty-six hours he feels so very hungry. If they don't give us food in Tallinn, the hunger will pass anyway. Without bread it's so very difficult to live, while with bread alone a person can be full up.'

A voice sounds from the corner of the waggon. 'If the engineer does not stop his prattling, I give him my word that I will open the door and fling him onto the track while we're going at full speed.'

The engineer mutters something about the harmony spread by beauty, goodness and progress, the victory afforded by hope over anger and the spiritual regeneration of louts.

It is now light outside. Professor Zemánek is quarrelling with the whole waggon, claiming that we must be at the coast because he can sense the salty sea air. Finally he observes that someone from our group has slipped into his pocket a whole shoal of fish-eggs taken from the rotten pickled herring that they distributed among us in their self-denying way at Narva.

Quite naturally he feels insulted. The engineer gently observes to him that to suffer the taunts of others is the greatest virtue. The world must become acquainted with the gospel of love.

Under pressure from several clearly-meant threats, the engineer buries himself in his coat and keeps quiet all the way to Kulmo, where all the male members of the transport set about breaking up a supply of peat and wood they managed to get hold of in order to heat the waggons.

When the robbers have returned with their ill-gotten gains and a fire is crackling merrily in the little stoves, the engineer crawls down from his perch and says:

'Misappropriating things that do not properly belong to you is theft and those who act in this way are nothing but common thieves. We must all answer for this. If I use stolen wood, coal or peat in order to keep myself warm, then I am complicit in thievery too.'

In the debate that follows in the wake of his protestations, it becomes clear that if he wasn't part of the raiding party he has no right to share in the spoils. If he wants to sit in the warm, he must go and steal a log.

'He who is to receive goods must also provide them.' They open the door for him and thrust him outside. 12 degrees of frost are there to greet him. A short while later he comes back bearing a sizeable log and says: 'I have taken something that is not mine; I am a thief.'

At the station in Kulmo word spreads that the representative of the Red Cross has stopped off at Mörigölje in order to negotiate by phone with the authorities in Tallinn. The news passes through all the waggons like a last flicker of hope, only to be extinguished by the scepticism expressed in the simple words of a Czech citizen from Smíchov: 'Yet another one of their rackets.' He was quite correct in his view. When we should already be pulling into the station at Tallinn, the train branches off onto the harbour line which by-passes in a huge curve the town itself, where we should be having 1: lunch, 2: dinner and 3: breakfast.

The train puts on speed as it carries us along the coastline. No one is paying any attention to the sea. They all turn back to look at the sandy banks of the cutting behind which the town of Tallinn hides its cowardly face and savours its lucky escape from the iron will of desperadoes.

The train comes to the end of the line. We have reached a pier and are alongside a cargo steamer called the *Cyprus*, while another steamer lies at anchor between us and the island of Silgit.

On the waterside a deputation from some association of Tallinn women and girls with a pastor at their head is waiting for us. They hand out newspapers from our homeland, while a choir of girls and women sings touchingly in German:

Those who worldly bliss would taste
Must keep from all the sins
Whoever is by death embraced
Inhales God's love and wins.

Half an hour later the pastor and his choir of ladies and girls have been dunked in the sea, while with a terrible cry of 'Hurrah!' we all make a beeline for the *Cyprus* moored by the pier.

V The crew of the *Cyprus*, for the most part experienced old sea dogs, gave us short shrift. It was like a shepherd counting sheep into a pen. They take hold of each sheep by its fleece and toss it in. Each person ran the gamut of a tourniquet as several pairs of hairy and brawny nautical arms passed him further down the line until he found himself somewhere below deck and assigned to one of the groups of ten now sprouting in the hold like mushrooms after rain. By the time that he'd recovered his senses he found himself with his group at a second exit in the other end of the boat. He received a loaf of bread, a tin of meat, a spoon, a metal plate and a cup and found himself back in his place in the hold. Within half an hour the whole group had been supplied, seated and satisfied.

The engineer finds his spirits returning and continues expounding: 'A person replete is a person content, but a hungry man can never achieve happiness.'

He has a very small audience around him, but this cannot prevent the unassailable outpourings from pouring out:

'Before we can set off the steamship will have to weigh anchor and they'll have to stoke the fires to get the boilers going. If it were a sailing ship, it would have to wait for a favourable wind. Without wind a sailing ship cannot move, just as a car can go nowhere without petrol.'

The *Cyprus* signals to the line of little steamboats supervising harbour traffic that we are on our way and a reply is signalled back: 'Your passage is clear'. With the steam turbines sending us on our way with a whistle, we say farewell to the banks of Estonia, enveloped in a rolling mist as if they wanted to say: 'There's no point in looking behind you, you've lived through nothing with us that's worth looking back on.'

All the same a few sentimental returnees wave dirty scarves. A group of Estonian boys and girls from the nearby fishing cabins stand on the pier and stick their tongues out at us. Three unshaven Tyroleans hold hands while they sing:

Wann ich kumm, wann ich kumm,
wann ich wieder, wieder kumm ...

I take a look at the notices on the boat. No one can doubt their ingenuity: 'Should you observe fire on board ship, inform a senior officer.' 'Access to the Captain's Bridge is forbidden to passengers and cargo.'

'The key to the store-room containing lifebelts is to be found with the junior officer to whom all mishaps must be reported.' Under this I managed to add: 'If the boat goes down, inform the captain.'

I go to spy out the canteens and a notice welcomes me like a knife thrust: 'The sale of alcoholic spirits is strictly forbidden.'

Where is the magic of that sailor's rum, that whisky, that grog? Where are those sozzled old sea dogs of Kipling's stories, who sang 'yo ho ho and a bottle of rum' as they drank their fill and more?

Instead they are selling oat beer, lemonade, sugarplums, gingerbread and chocolate, as if schoolchildren were enjoying a trip under the supervision of their teachers at the end of the school year.

There was a second canteen at the other end of the ship, which painted the same bleak picture, as if the hand of Dr. Foustka or Professor Batěk, those teetotaling quacks, was behind it. On offer were lemons, apples, pickled herring, sardines in oil, tinned fish and postcards. You could also get some vile German cigarettes and cigars that were even worse.

I continue my tour of the ship and discover another batch of notices dealing with the lifeboats and the procedures for lowering them into the water. One lifeboat particularly interests me. There is a hole of some size in the bottom of it. Then I inspect the sailors' cabins. Their inhabitants are drinking coffee, they are perfectly sober, their mouths are free of clay pipes. In the hands of one of them is a thick book with the pages edged in red. I suspect it of being a Bible. I close the door quietly, having apologised for the intrusion, and go to breathe in the fresh air at the prow of the boat, where at that very moment they are signalling to a boat carrying Russian prisoners back to their homeland.

Everyone clambers out onto the deck. On the boat with the Russians they produce a scarlet banner.

The boats come alongside each other in order and communicate. We and they are waving scarves and shouting 'Urra!' while here and there tears well up in eyes and no one is ashamed to be seen with them.

Mutual greetings skim the surface of the open sea in the gulf, only to be carried back as they echo off the chalk cliffs of the island of Silgit opposite.

In the gulf the surface is calm. Gulls hover above the sea before they drop and dive.

The engineer has words of wisdom to offer as ever:

'The word we use in Czech to denote the black-haired gull literally means 'giggling gull', because its cry suggests the sound of human laughter. If it did not laugh...'

'In that case I would throw you overboard,' I add in a serious tone.

We skirt the long shoreline of some land or other and the engineer explains in forthright terms: 'That is an island, because it is surrounded by water on all sides. But suppose the shoreline of the land in question were to be connected to the mainland on one side or other. That would make it a peninsula.' A circle of listeners forms around the engineer. He indicates the fishing boats in the gulf and makes another irrefutable pronouncement:

'The sea teems with fish and fishing is the only form of employment in which fishermen engage. The diet of many fish consists of other fish, which were this not the case would mean their dying of hunger. The shark is a dangerous creature for people who are bathing in the sea. The sea is deep in places, although in other places it is shallow. Sea water has a salty character.'

The listeners hoist the engineer high off the ground and dangle him over the surface of the sea. He cries out: 'If you let go of me, I'll drown.' Someone fetches a bucket of sea water. They stretch the engineer out on the deck and soak him with water before taking him away to dry off in the boiler-room. He is so taken aback that not a single word of wisdom springs to his mind, and one only appears at dinner time, when he mentions in passing: 'A pea stays round even when boiled.'

This is the gospel truth, but the pea in question, which they gave us in the soup, must have been on strike when they were boiling it because it is as hard as the Charles Bridge.

Another pleasant surprise about the soup was the presence of prunes, apples, oat bran and salty fish eggs.

Just imagine that most of us had already eaten a cold tin of greasy meat, a slab of chocolate or marzipan, apples, marinated herring, pickled onions and sardines in the canteen, washed down with oat beer and lemonade.

It provided the best of preparations for the seasickness lying in wait somewhere over the horizon of the open sea.

Black night fell upon us. Lighthouses glowed in the darkness on the island of Silgit and a north-westerly wind began to gather strength. Once we'd left the shelter of the gulf the waves did not wait upon their coming but announced themselves at once, in the full force of their rage.

The *Cyprus* began to slice through the waves, which broke the silence of the night with their cries of pain and in their fury tried to drown the ship, to drive her into the depths of the sea.

The *Cyprus* performed such a cake walk on the waves that we were really taken ill by it. A sense of fellowfeeling spread throughout the ranks. Every stomach was being held, with no distinction according to creed, country or conviction or, as Professor Zemánek put it so well, 'I think I've had a bellyful of this.'

All writers who describe a voyage by sea mention sea sickness and make heroes of themselves. Everyone is sick save one – the scribbler. There is one honourable exception to this rule, for I was among the afflicted. In fact I was so badly affected that for the first time in my life I turned my thoughts to the Lord God and uttered an earnest prayer above the roar of the waves:

'Almighty God, I draw near to you in spirit and if truth be told I long to speak with you, although you can see what I'm doing right now. You created me to give praise to you in your glory and you show compassion to me in my wretchedness. I promise you that with your help I will put myself at the service of your law, renouncing all forms of heresy and depravity. I do not wish to be in harness with unbelievers and godless types. I will send word to Bohemia and write a poem of praise to the papal nuncio.'

The upshot was that I entered the following in my diary with a trembling hand: 'Things go from bad to worse. So much for prayer.'

As it set over the raging sea, the sun discovered us in the very same position leaning over the handrail, and that's how we stayed all night.

The engineer, his head next to mine while he leaned over the waves, observed in a whisper: 'Sea sickness is not to be found on dry land.'

Poor wretch that I was, I didn't even have the strength to throw him overboard as a sacrificial victim to placate an angry sea.

VI The practical effects of those bodily motions which scientists and laymen alike define as sea sickness lasted for a full thirty-six hours. There was nothing to be cheerful about on board the boat because no one, including the captain, knew exactly where we were going.

He claimed that the boat had no choice but to meet the waves head on. It's true that no one could object to this, but the problem was that the wind and waves kept changing direction, with the result that we zigzagged along like a pirate ship dodging cannonfire from the coast.

The cake walk resumed towards evening of the second day, and this time things were even worse. We all wished for some way of putting an end to it all.

The captain comforted us with the observation that we'd seen nothing yet, and that he'd once had to maintain a lurching rhythm carving his way through the waves for a whole fortnight. In all that time he only managed to cover a short distance between Danzig and Riga, and now we were trying to make it all the way from Tallinn to Stettin.

Slowly we grew used to sea sickness and even began to find an appetite for that famous soup of the old German Reich based upon prunes and overcooked sardines.

Towards morning the engineer showed up on deck and began to shout: 'Land Ahoy!' The same cry was probably uttered by the sailor in the crow's nest on the *Santa Maria* when Columbus discovered America. Even our teachers taught us about the sailor shouting 'Land Ahoy!' The engineer knew the whole story by heart and now made his own use of an historic saying, yelling 'Land Ahoy!' yet again.

We asked the captain about our whereabouts. After a long time spent searching and measuring, he announced that we were near the Danish coast or the Swedish coast, unless we were near one of the islands belonging to one or the other of these two kingdoms.

The precise identification of where we were proved to be a source of general excitement. Some woman dissolved in tears at the fact that she would not see Germany again on account of our not heading towards Stettin but to the opposite shoreline.

Making my way through a crowd of flustered people I offered my own halfpennyworth. I suggested that the boat was taking us to America.

Fortunately the wind changed direction once more and the *Cyprus* was compelled to slice through the waves in a southerly direction, heading for Germany. However, this was not the end of it and in the course of that day we headed to the South-East, North-East, in a southerly direction once again, then North-West and finally South-West.

The engineer on his straw mattress below deck wondered out loud: 'With the invention of the compass ships are able to determine which direction is South, North, West and East. The South Pole lies to the South, whilst the North Pole, on the other hand, lies to the North.' The woman who had been in tears when we were 'either alongside Denmark or Sweden' now had a fit of hysteria and yelled that in no way was she going to the North Pole, a place that filled her with dread.

However, the engineer would not allow himself to be interrupted and continued to hold forth: 'The West Pole and the East Pole do not exist, meaning that there are only two, the South and the North, just as there are two hemispheres, the Southern and the Northern. We belong to the Northern hemisphere, and if there were Australians among our ranks, we would have people on board belonging to the Southern hemisphere. The world is round and turns on its axis unceasingly, day after day, year after year. If we are in Stettin tomorrow, that will mean that we have arrived safely and that Stettin is a port.' He paused to drink his oat beer and under the glare of hostile glances went off to sleep.

The following night the wind disappeared. The *Cyprus* no longer had its work cut out slicing through the waves and steamed along contentedly. The captain set course for Swinemünde, the sky cleared and towards noon the seagulls began to return. The horizon ahead did not dance in front of our eyes any more. In fact the water was as calm and quiet as one of the ponds around Prague.

In the afternoon we saw a shoreline made up of dense pine forests on low hills, and it was still light when we arrived in Swinemünde with its lighthouse, its fishing business, its abandoned spas and its barracks once full of sailors, whose numbers nowadays could be counted on the fingers of one hand.

This great fortified military dockyard was the pride of Germany and now lies in ruins. The Germans had to blow it to smithereens, just like their imperious dreadnoughts, whose broken parts lie strewn around the wreckage of the port today.

Nevertheless, there simply must be a band on the bank. It is an old military band, and it welcomes us to Prussian Pomerania at the mouth of the River Swina where it runs into the Baltic Sea.

Looking at the ruins, the engineer could not refrain from comment: 'A scuttled warship is no longer of any use. Because this is where the River Swina debouches into the sea, and because in German the mouth of a river is called Münde, this place is – and quite correctly – called Swinemünde, meaning mouth of the Swina. If it was mouth of what we call the Labe and the Germans the Elbe, why then it would be Elbemünde. And if it was the mouth of the Rýn as we call it, or the Rhein as the Germans say, why then it would be Rheinmünde. After all, it's only logical.'

The ship moves through the Oder Canal which connects the port with the town of Stettin, inducing the engineer to produce another piece of logic: 'If there was no Oder, Stettin would no longer be the largest commercial port in Prussia and we would be forced to go there by train rather than on water, and without water they could not build any ships here. For this reason we can say that the Oder has done Stettin a good turn.'

We were delivered from these erudite reflections by the rumbling of a dropped anchor. We are to stay here awhile and have to undergo examination by the Board of Health.

When the members of this body arrived, they took us before the Board one by one. They are not people to make a song and dance of it. They ask you to poke out your tongue, and that's it.

When several hundred prisoners-of-war had treated the illustrious Board of Health to their tongues, it pronounced itself satisfied and went away. We weighed anchor. The band on the bank then treated us to 'Heil dir im Siegerkranz' and we are now continuing along the Oder Canal to the Pomeranian capital. Apparently a lavish reception is on the cards.

HOW I CAME TO MEET THE AUTHOR OF MY OBITUARY

In the course of the five or six years when I was living in Russia I was on several occasions randomly killed and put down by various individuals and organisations.

When I returned to my own country, I discovered that I'd been hanged three times, shot twice and on one occasion quartered by savage Kyrgyz rebels near Lake Issyk-Kul.

Last but not least, my life came to a definitive end when I was run through in a wild affray with drunken sailors in one of Odessa's ale-houses. This seems the likeliest version to me too.

My good friend Kolmanov took the same view. Having obtained an eye-witness report of my valiant if ignominious demise, he wrote the whole (to me highly unpleasant) affair up in an article for the editor of his journal.

However, he did not make do with a minor news bulletin. His big heart impelled him to write my obituary, which I read shortly after my return to Prague.

Convinced as he was that the dead do not come back from the grave, he besmirched my posthumous reputation in the most elegant of terms.

In order to persuade him that I was in the land of the living, I went to seek him out, and so begins this tale.

Even that master of the macabre Edgar Allan Poe could not have thought up a more grisly theme for a story.

I found the author of my obituary in one of Prague's wine bars on the stroke of midnight, the hour when it shuts its doors in accordance with some imperial ruling dating from the 18th April, 1856.

His eyes were fixed on the ceiling. The tables were being relieved of their stained tablecloths. I sat down at his and said in an affable way: 'Permit me to ask whether this seat is free.'

He went on scrutinising some unrecognisable mark on the ceiling which seemed to have captured his interest, before replying in a reasonable enough way: 'It is, but the place is about to close; I doubt whether they'll serve you.'

I took hold of his arm and forced him to face me. He spent a while observing me without a word. Finally he said in a quiet voice: 'Excuse me, but haven't you been in Russia?'

I laughed: 'You recognise me, then? I was killed in a low Russian dive, brawling with some rough drunken sailors.'

The colour went out of him. 'You are... you are....'

'Exactly right,' I said emphatically, 'I was killed by sailors in a tavern in Odessa and in the light of my death you wrote my obituary.'

Words came in the form of a faintly audible gasp:

'You've read what I wrote about you?'

'Naturally. It's a very interesting obituary, apart from one or two little misunderstandings. And unusually long into the bargain. Even His Imperial Highness received fewer lines upon His royal decease. Your magazine devoted 152 lines to him and 186 to myself. At 35 hellers a line (how miserable a pittance they used to give journalists) that makes 55 crowns and 15 hellers in all.'

'What exactly do you want from me?' he asked in panic. 'Do you want those 55 crowns and 15 hellers?'

'Keep your money,' I replied, 'the dead do not demand a fee for their obituaries.'

The colour continued to drain away from his cheeks.

'You know what,' I said casually, 'We'll pay up and drop in elsewhere. I want to spend tonight with you.'

'Couldn't it wait until tomorrow?' I fixed him with a cold stare.

'The bill,' he called out.

Having summoned a horse and carriage from the corner of the street, I bade the author of my obituary take a seat, while to the driver I said in a sepulchral tone:

'Take us to the Olšany cemetery!'

The one who penned my death notice proceeded to make the sign of the cross. A long and painful silence reigned in the carriage, broken only by the crack of the coachman's whip and the snorting of his horses.

I leaned over to my companion and said: 'Have you noticed how the howling of the dogs punctures the silence of these quiet suburban streets?'

He shuddered, stood up in the carriage and managed to stammer: 'You were really in Russia?'

'Killed in one of Odessa's ale-houses. Had a scrap with some drunken sailors,' I replied drily.

'Holy Mary!' came the response from my companion, 'this is worse than *The Spectre's Bride*.'

The painful silence returned. From somewhere around a dog really did bark.

When we reached the main road in Strašnice, I told my companion to pay the driver. There we were standing in the darkness of the highway. Completely and pitiably at a loss, the author of my obituary turned to me and said: 'Do you think there might be a restaurant around here somewhere?'

'A restaurant?' I laughed. 'What we are now going to do is scale the wall of the cemetery. Then we are going to find a gravestone somewhere in order to have a chat about your obituary. You can climb on ahead and give me a hand up.'

Without a word he gave me his hand and we jumped down into the cemetery. Low branches of the cypress bushes crackled beneath our feet. There was a melancholy murmur of wind among the crosses.

'I am not going any further,' he blurted out. 'Just where are you taking me?'

'What we are going to do now,' I said cheerfully as I propped him up, 'is have a look at the tomb of an old Prague patrician family called Bonepiani. There is a grave in the first section of row six by the wall which has been completely abandoned. Abandoned from the moment when they laid to rest there the last of their descendants, who was transported in 1874 from Odessa, where he was killed by sailors in a low tavern brawl.'

Once again my companion crossed himself.

At last we were sitting beside the gravestone covering the dust that made up the mortal remains of the last descendants of the Bonepiani, citizens of Prague. That was when I gently took the author of my death notice by the hand and began to explain in a quiet voice:

'My dear friend! When we were at junior high school our esteemed teachers taught us a beautiful and lofty principle: *De mortuis nil nisi bonum.* You, on the other hand, have tried to write about me, a dead person, in the worst possible terms. If I were to write that obituary myself, I would write that never did a person leave behind such sadness at his passing than was occasioned by the death of Whatshisname. I would write that the most splendid virtue of the dead writer was his active love of all that is good and of all that is sacred to those of a pure soul like him. But you have written of my death that a rogue and buffoon had passed away unmourned! Stop crying! There are occasions when the heart savours the opportunity to write about the most pleasant moments in the life of one who has now passed away. But you have written that the deceased was an alcoholic.'

The author of my obituary gave himself over to a fresh bout of crying, which carried an air of melancholy across the peace of the cemetery and was lost somewhere in the distance near the park with the Jewish furnaces.

'Dear friend', I said forcefully, 'do not cry, it's too late to put things right now...'

Having spoken these words I proceeded to vault over the cemetery wall and ran down to the gatekeeper. I rang the bell and announced that I was returning from putting in some overtime night duty at work when I heard crying behind the cemetery wall, somewhere in the first section.

'Some well-oiled widower,' replied the gatekeeper cynically, 'We'll have him locked up.'

I waited by the corner. About ten minutes later some of the security guards were escorting the author of my obituary to the guardhouse.

He was shouting as he struggled with them: 'Am I dreaming or is this really happening? Gentlemen, are you acquainted with the story of *The Spectre's Bride*?'

THE FUN OF JAROSLAV HAŠEK (1883-1923)*

JAROSLAV HAŠEK was not an educated man, but a rather clever man with an exceptionally good memory. He did get into grammar school (*Gymnasium*), but had to leave in the fourth form because he did not meet the grade. His schoolmaster father's death after an operation in 1896 had no doubt had a considerable impact on his ability to study. He then started work as a pharmacist's apprentice, but not long after that he began to attend the Czecho-Slav Commercial Academy in Prague; while at this school, one of his masters came to believe that he would become the Czech Mark Twain, and Hašek published his first short story in 1901. From the age of eighteen to his death, that is, in twenty-two years, he wrote some 1,500 short stories. Although by far his best known work is the unfinished *Fortunes of the Good Soldier Švejk in the Great War* (1921–23), his strength remained in the short story.

Indeed, that is evident from the novel, where the chief function of the main character, Švejk, is to tell often still very funny stories and to engineer, or land up in, funny situations. The novel's actual narrative is, generally, tedious and rambling and its language is for the time somewhat archaic Czech. Furthermore, putting the Švejk character into a novel that is, at least attempting to make a round

*) In this afterword, for the sake of the reader, I do my best to restrict myself to comparing the Bugulma stories with works that have been translated into English, that is, the Švejk works and *A Tourist Guide*. Švej*k in Captivity* is the exception (as far as I can ascertain). My translations of the titles of Hašek works are literal and therefore may not always correspond exactly with those of the various translators. Normal British English until the late 1940s, for example, was the 'Great War', while the Second World War was called the 'World War' (I strive not to be anachronistic).

character of him, fails.* Indeed, Švejk becomes, to put it mildly, not at all the sort of fellow you might like as a friend: he lacks compassion of any sort; his fearlessness reminds one far more of a large postmodern thug than of a courageous soldier; he is physically violent, enjoys brawls, is sarcastic, impertinent, mendacious, a trickster and a bully, who believes that noble behaviour belongs only in novels. On the other hand, he is quick-witted, street-wise, not only unbulliable, but also indestructible, indeed altogether the very model of a twenty-first-century ideal – he is attractive to women, too, especially because of his well-developed thighs. I find it difficult to think of the work as an anti-war novel, as the Left did long before Communism overtook Czechoslovakia. It is certainly anti-Austrian (but Austria had disintegrated before it was published, and so there was little point in satirising that state any more), but if one were determined to find some message, it would surely be that if you adopt Švejkian optimism and impervious loutishness, even war can be a fun game.

That suggests that something complicated is going on, for Hašek himself was recommended for an Austrian medal for gallantry shortly before he had gone over to the Russian side (he allowed himself to be captured). He received his call-up papers in 1915, and in the same year he ended in a Russian P.O.W. camp. In 1916 he joined the central offices of the Czechoslovak Brigade that was under Russian command and, in the same year, took part in the battle of Zborów, where his conduct led to his being awarded a tsarist Rus-

*) Rather than have him the main character of short stories as in the collection *The Good Soldier Švejk and Other Strange Tales* [1912], republished between the wars as *The Good Soldier Švejk Before the War and Other Strange Tales* [1922, 1926], or even in the brief, sarcastic novel *The Good Soldier Švejk in Captivity* (1917 in Kiev, 2nd and 3rd editions in 1947 and 1948 no doubt on account of its misoteutonism).

sian medal for gallantry. In his writing for the Brigade (and then the 'legion'* which passed under French command), he generally shared the Czech nationalist and pan-Slav bigotry of most of the 'legionary' writers and journalists. He turned down, however, the ideals of the new 'legion'. In the Spring of 1918, Hašek followed his political convictions of the time by leaving Ukraine for Moscow, where he joined the left wing of the Czech Social Democrats, that is, the Czech section of the Bolsheviks. He had, then, betrayed his country twice, once by going over to the Russians and once by abandoning the 'legion'. One must not, however, underestimate his bravery in joining Red military activities, willingly accepting the Party's making him assistant to the officer in command in Bugulma: if during his time with the Reds he had encountered Czechoslovak legionaries, he would have been executed, and probably tortured beforehand – however popular he had been as a man and a writer when he was in Kiev. When Hašek is mentioned at all in any of the right-wing legionary novels that I have read, it is with affection – which is not the case with his Švejk (though Švejk does appear in left-wing anti-war novels). It is certainly misleading of the best-informed of today's students of Hašek, Radko Pytlík, to entitle his afterword to the Czech edition of this book 'Švejk in Tatar Bugulma'. Gašek (Gashek)** has very few of Švejk's characteristics and Gašek is not Hašek either, but an ironic, sometimes more or less grotesque,

*) I use inverted commas because these soldiers regarded themselves as the Czechoslovak Army, and were initially offended on returning from Siberia to the new Czechoslovak state to learn that they were labelled 'legionaries', which was especially shocking for a 'hero of Zborów', for even before the soldiers returned home, this battle had become a corner-stone of the new country's foundation myth.

**) Russians have 'G' for Czech, or indeed most English, names beginning with H.

version of the author – though most of the events described in the stories presented did take place, even the episode concerning barracks-cleaning nuns, but Hašek's intention is satire, not verisimilitude. Satire often entails turning things upside down, just as it entails sarcasm, elsewhere considered the lowest form of wit. Probably the account of the vicissitudes of refugees'/repatriates' journey from the northern Baltic to Germany comes closest to verisimilitude. Satirists also frequently enjoy types, and the know-all who thrusts his banal knowledge on everyone within earshot is one of the most vivid types in the present collection, for he reminds one of people the reader has encountered all over the world. Hašek returned to Prague in 1920.

The Bugulma stories were freely available during the Communist era in Czechoslovakia, though given the distorted book supply system, it was often almost impossible to find individual volumes from the Works (1955–74). Still, the exile publishing house in Toronto, 68 Publishers, published the Bugulma stories in 1976, a shorter collection than the present, and many copies were smuggled into Czechoslovakia. In 1981, Cecil Parrott's translations of eight of the stories contained in the present volume were published in his *The Red Commissar*. The editors of the present version hope that some readers will have the time to compare the two translations.

In the Bugulma stories Hašek has returned to many of the comic techniques of his pre-war short stories, though the slapstick of which he had been a master is greatly diminished and in the present stories the author makes proportionately greater use of what is normally called antithetical hyperbole (satire achieved by means of an exaggeration of horror or evil by portraying the opposite of the actual state of affairs, closer to collusive irony than to sarcasm) than in his pre-war stories. For nearly every episode in these stories Hašek as narrator looks like the opposite of the war-time, more or less stock central European antisemite nationalist, national and, subsequently Communist propagandist. I am not saying there is absolutely nothing left of the old (or, indeed, the post-war) comic writer in the war-time writing, but on the whole, he is a coarser and simultaneously more conventional writer, even in *The Good Soldier Švejk in Captivity*. But then, even *The Fortunes of the Good Soldier Švejk in the Great War* is coarser than the pre-war short stories, and, indeed, than the Bugulma stories. These stories, with some exceptions, manifest Hašek's old fascination with, indeed often affection for, outsider groups, here Tatars, Buryats (it is said that Hašek founded Buryat journalism), Circassians and other non-Russians. Only the Chinese are a major exception, for some of his writing on them is essentially racist. That racism may be contrasted with a story from the pre-war collection, *A Tourist Guide* (1913), where, after he has been converted to Christianity, a clever Chinese has the priest who had converted him executed so that his desire for eternal life in Heaven can be fulfilled as soon as possible. Hašek also had a weak spot for Gypsies, but that is not evident in the Bugulma stories. In his pre-war writing, on the whole, he had an equally weak spot for Jews; one thinks of his story about the failure to realise a Jewish arranged marriage, which works just as well as another, also set in Galicia, that presents a more or less slapstick satire on Hasidic miraculous rabbis or messiahs, again narrated with great warmth. In this last story a messiah is never seen chewing onions while walking, which is ambivalent, for it is difficult to tell whether Hašek is using a central European antisemitic stereotype – that Jews always stink of onions or garlic or both, or in fact making fun of that stereotype. That ambivalence becomes particularly clear if we turn to the Chinese story in the present collection ('Chzhen-si, the Supreme Truth'), for here, when a Chinese and a Korean leave the narrator's room, leaving behind them the smell of 'garlic and beaver butter', Hašek is certainly making fun of antisemitic stereotyping as well as of the well-nigh universal folk convention that foreigners smell different (naturally, not because of distinctive types of eau de Cologne). If my ignorance has become clear in that I am unaware that beaver butter was Davy Crockett's caviar, it does not affect my view on the function of this particular stench. In *The Fortunes*, something similar, though a little more complex, is going on in the non-antisemitic portrayal of padre Katz, a likeable rogue for Švejk and probably most readers. At first sight, it might look grotesque to have a Jew as a Roman Catholic padre, but, for example, Theodor Kohn was the influential Archbishop of Olomouc, 1892–1904. On the other hand, in spite of the efforts of the Catholic modernists, the Roman Church in Austria contained a viciously antisemitic element, whose most prolific representative was Rudolf Vrba. Thus the figure of Katz could embody political satire that goes far beyond the stock anticlericalism of Czech liberals and socialists of Hašek's day. Simultaneously, and this may be the most significant aspect of the Katz portrait, Hašek is mocking the antisemitic stereotypes of Jews as procuring during the war only cushy behind-the-lines jobs, of being too clumsy to handle weapons, and, indeed, of being cowards. Something not quite so complex occurs in the Bugulma stories with the visit of three members of the Revolutionary Tribunal of the Eastern Front.

Two of the three have names that indicate that they are Jewish, even though, perhaps, these names are Hašek's invention. The antisemitic notion of Jews as revolutionaries in Russia was present in Czech literature at least two decades before the outbreak of war, and in Austria the Social Democrat leadership did indeed contain many Jews; in Rudolf Vrba and the antisemitic faction of the Church, Marxism was considered an altogether dangerous ideology invented by a Jew for the good of the Jews and their desire to increase their power in the world, thus to disrupt the glorious order of the Monarchy. In Czech literature, as far as I know the first portrayal of a Jew wanting to replace the present devices of the Jews to achieve world domination, running finance and the press, by a device of instigating a violent social revolution all over Europe and North America, comes in the first entirely antisemitic Czech novel, a three-part work, where rich Jews are ritual murderers, criminals, poisoners and white-slave traders, and, in keeping with an old topos of antisemitism, the financially most powerful of the whole group of conspirators turns out to be an Irish noble of part-elvan descent, a Christian stolen as an infant by the eminence grise of the whole Jewish conspiracy to rule the world. This novel, *A Conspiracy of Jews in Prague* (1873), was written by the particularly minor writer Eduard Rüffer. The female member of Hašek's Revolutionary Tribunal has the un-Russian name Kalibanova. The word *kaliban* was used, more in the nineteenth century than later, to mean simply an unsightly monster as it (Caliban) was in English. Rüffer uses it only of his Jews. I am not suggesting that Hašek knew Rüffer's novel, but he could have done, for he liked trash literature and enjoyed using its topoi and sometimes its style as a satirical device. Kalibanova's name suggests ugliness to the Czech reader and so, typical of his humour, Hašek labels her 'pleasant, vivacious'. The second Jew is Agapov, and his un-Russian name indicates something akin to the satirical Christian-cum-Jewish portrait of padre Katz. At the time of writing, agape, love, meant primarily either the love feast that attended Holy Communion, when gifts for the poor were assembled, or simply Christian love (the Roman Catholics' *caritas*). Hašek's Agapov is a bitter, vengeful character, 'cruel, inexorable, hard'. In another writer, such a tribunal would be most likely to act out a kangaroo court and punish Gašek severely or at least the stereotypical Russian Jerachymov (Yerakhimov) (hard-drinking, one moment gentle, affectionate, the next out to kill you – a stereotypical assessment of the Russian character at least since the Romantic period), once the delegation has discovered that Jerachymov had been drinking when he summoned the Tribunal by telegram to try Gašek. The portrayal of Kalibanova and Agapov actually appears to be mocking the concept Judaeobolshevism, and one is reminded of Hašek's pre-war story mocking the Catholic antisemitic picture of Jews exploiting farmers by leading them to mortgage their lands for the sake of drink; there the farmers rather than the Jewish publicans are to blame. In Bugulma the Tribunal is fair, and kind, and so makes for another example of Hašek's antithetical hyperbole.

This term applies to most of what Hašek describes of revolutionary activity. Gašek is able to take Bugulma and then become officer in command there with no violence whatsoever. Indeed, the mayor and citizens come to welcome the Communists with bread and salt (at the time it was considered an ancient Slav, including Czech, custom thus to welcome strangers to a town or a house, and one cannot know whether or not Hašek knew that the Irish considered it primordially Irish or Celtic). Equally unrealistic is the Bugulmans' willing, immediate, and complete compliance with Gašek's command that all weapons be handed in at his office. Gašek becomes a decent bureaucrat and is successful in his immediate institution of literacy classes, and eventually in getting a large body of nuns to leave their convent and clean the barracks in preparation for the arrival of a large Red Army contingent. Hašek's readers will have known the fates of thousands of nuns during the revolution and the civil war. The whole idea of bureaucracy functioning so well with so much public compliance is antithetical hyperbole. Hašek had satirised and would later consistently satirise chiefly Austrian bureaucracy, a fine example of which is the short story that portrays the complicated bureaucracy that controls matters in Purgatory. His picture of a revolutionary idyll in Russia is analogous to his pre-war short story about the extreme kindness and generosity of Bavarian policemen, prison warders and judges.

Nineteenth- and early twentieth-century Czech antisemitism is normally closely linked with nationalism. In Rüffer's case the concentration lies, however, on Jewish ritual murder of Christian children, not at all linked with Passover matzos, and on the Jewish plot to conquer the world; the only aspects of the novel that suggest some patriotism lie in the initial picture of the orphaned son and daughter of a Czech patriot from 1848 who are abducted by a brutish Jew but rescued by the Jew who turned out to be an Irish Christian, in the portrayal of the patriotic consumptive Libuše, and in the frequent use of the nationalist cliché which states that Bohemia or Prague is the heart of Europe. Hašek may have bowed to Czech patriotic antisemitism in his Czech war-time works (the most obvious example of that occurs at the beginning of *Švejk in Captivity*, the author's employment of the popular interpretation of the letters FJI [Franz Joseph I] on soldiers' caps as meaning 'Für jüdische Interessen', 'In Jewish interests', reflecting the myth that Rüffer exploits in an extreme fashion, that Jews cause wars in order to profit from them financially). Still, overall Hašek dislikes antisemitism as much as he dislikes conventional nationalism, all part of his anarchist mistrust of all well-established institutions. The first president of Czechoslovakia, T. G. Masaryk, and his Realist Party were institutions before the war and thus targets of Hašek's satire, which actually explains why the one sentence on Masaryk's organising a Czechoslovak army in Russia in *The Fortunes* is so innocuous; after the war Hašek will have nothing to do with the idolatry of the president that attended the First Republic. In the account of Gašek's exit from Russia one encounters half-hidden satire on Masarykian ideas in the tedious know-all engineer's words on 'the harmony of beauty, good and progress', the notion that 'hope lends the soul victory over swearing', on 'spiritual revival' and in his statement that 'The world must have a gospel of love'. Hašek may well be having a dig at Masarykian Realists with his mockery of teetotalism, which he associates with vegetarianism and the study of Esperanto. In the Švejk short-story collection, he uses comically the term 'moral insanity' in English, a term that Masaryk introduced into Czech and employed frequently. The third member of the Revolutionary Tribunal, the Russian with a common Russian name, Sorokin, speaks of 'the green viper of alcoholism' like both a Red commissar and a Masarykian Realist: the term is a stock phrase of the contemporary Czech temperance movement. (Hašek began drinking again on his return from Russia; while with the Communists he appears to have succeeded in not touching a drop.) In the pre-war story about the mentally challenged enthusiast Šeferna, Hašek satirises conventional unthinking nationalism, the ignorant cult of the early fifteenth-century Hussite warriors by Šeferna's love for his third-of-a-litre beer glass 'on which there glisten a Bohemian lion, a mace [the weapon], a flail [as weapon], and broken chains'. When Hašek sees the citizens of Bugulma walking in a column towards him with bread and salt, he feels like the Hussite warleader, Jan Žižka. Here Hašek is ironising Gašek's and his own role, but at the same time mocking mechanical nationalism, no doubt especially that of the Czechoslovak legionary leaders in Russia who named their regiments after not only Žižka, but also other leaders of the Hussite period. The nationalist version of Hussitism was another institution the anti-authoritarian Hašek was impelled to laugh at.

No doubt Hašek had been attracted to the anti-authoritarian aspect of Russian Communist ideology, but the Bugulma stories demonstrate that he had no time for the institutionalised arbitrary violence of the Russian civil war. The last story in this volume, where Gašek, now much closer to the real Hašek, takes his revenge on the journalist and poet Jaroslav Kolman-Cassius, who had, in real life, published an obituary of Hašek, as having died in an Odessa pub brawl, more than anything else informs us that Hašek still condoned individual rowdyism, whatever he thought of the rowdy Red and White Armies and perhaps also of the ultimately anti-Red violence of the Czechoslovak Army in Russia, the 'legions'. That was not fun.

Robert B. Pynsent

TRANSLATOR'S NOTE AND ACKNOWLEDGEMENT

In this translation I have made a number of decisions which by definition cannot please everyone. My only hope is that those who think them mistaken will still enjoy the translation.

One thing I have done is to give modern names to a number of the places referred to (for instance Tallinn, St Petersburg), on the grounds that it provides the general reader with better orientation. But could I really give Simbirsk the name (Ulyanovsk) which it later acquired and has since retained as Lenin's birthplace? I could not. It would make more for disorientation than orientation to have updated it. Overall, I have updated where I have thought it appropriate.

There are a range of languages involved in the text – besides Czech there are quotations and wordplays involving German, Hungarian, Russian and Chinese, to name but four. Sometimes I have left quotations in the original, sometimes I have translated them – again, I have done so where I thought it appropriate. I have no knowledge of Chinese whatsoever, and therefore my English rendering of the names and sayings would have been pure guesswork were it not for the invaluable assistance of Dušan Andrš.

I wish to thank Martin Janeček for his editorial assistance and, as ever, my murderously meticulous wife, Lenka Cornerová Zdráhalová, for going through the text with a toothcomb, if not a razor. Thanks are also due to Lucie Johnová for many suggestions and significant improvements.

EDITOR'S NOTE

This volume represents a new selection of Hašek short stories. They have been arranged by the editor in a chronological order corresponding to the author's own life-history. The text used for translation is drawn from the fourth edition of the "Selected Works of Jaroslav Hašek" (*Třetí dekameron. Reelní podnik*), published in Prague by the Československý spisovatel publishing house in 1977 under the editorship of Radko Pytlík, using as reference also the texts published in the series "Works of Jaroslav Hašek" produced by the SNKLHU and Československý spisovatel publishing house between 1955 and 1968. To run in parallel with the English translation, this collection of short stories is also being published in the original Czech.

CONTENTS

Central European modern history is notable for many political and cultural discontinuities and often violent changes as well as many attempts to preserve and (re)invent traditional cultural identities. This series cultivates contemporary translations of influential literary works into English (and other languages) which have not been available to global readership due to censorship, the effects of Cold War or repetitive political disruptions in Czech publishing and its international ties.

Readers in English both in today's cosmopolitan Prague or anywhere in the physical and electronic world can thus become acquainted with works which capture the Central European historical experience and which express and also have helped to form Czech and Central European nature, humour and imagination.

Believing that any literary canon can be defined only in dialogue with other cultures, the series will bring proven classics used in Western university courses as well as (re)discoveries aiming to provide new perspectives in intermedial areal studies of literature, history and culture.

All titles are accompanied by an afterword, the translations are reviewed and circulated in the scholarly community before publication which has been reflected by nominations for several literary awards.

Modern Czech Classics series edited by Martin Janeček
and Karolinum Press

Published titles
Zdeněk Jirotka: Saturnin (2003, 2005, 2009, 2013; pb 2016)
Vladislav Vančura: Summer of Caprice (2006; pb 2016)
Karel Poláček: We Were a Handful (2007; pb 2016)
Bohumil Hrabal: Pirouettes on a Postage Stamp (2008)
Karel Michal: Everyday Spooks (2008)
Eduard Bass: The Chattertooth Eleven (2009)
Jaroslav Hašek: Behind the Lines. Bugulma and Other Stories (2012; pb 2016)
Bohumil Hrabal: Rambling On (2014; pb 2016)
Ladislav Fuks: Of Mice and Mooshaber (2014)
Josef Jedlička: Midway Upon the Journey of Our Life (2016)
Jaroslav Durych: God's Rainbow (2016)

In Translation
Ladislav Fuks: The Cremator
Bohuslav Reynek: The Well at Morning
Ludvík Vaculík: Czech Dreambook
Jan Čep: Short Stories